Laurence,
Best wishes to
a fellow writer!
Lesley Waite

WALKING ON
TRAIN TRACKS

LESLEY MEIROVITZ WAITE

D0869240

This book is a work of fiction. Names, characters, places, and incidents are either the product of the author's imagination or are used fictitiously. Any resemblance to actual persons, living or dead, events, or locales is entirely coincidental.

cover photo by Tom Buchbinder
author photo by Karen Siff Exkorn

Copyright © 2013 Lesley Meirovitz Waite

All rights reserved.

ISBN: 0615664881

ISBN-13: 9780615664880

To Miles and Casey with love
Special thanks to my beloved Tom and my writing buddy
Karen for their love, inspiration and encouragement.

She wrote on walls with a Sharpie, she walked on train tracks with a swagger, she contained everything in her pocket. She pictured everyone watching her like a camera.

CHAPTER ONE

The Boy at Crystal Lake

On April 15, 1978, the day started with a cracked mirror. In a metaphoric sense.

My parents were banging on the bathroom door. My sister had locked herself inside. Again.

"Open the door!" My mom was beating down the door. "You open the door right now!"

Silence. Mom turned to Dad. "You talk to her."

"Jessie, we mean it. Open up. Now."

Mom's voice was shaky. "She won't eat anything. It's just a protein shake, the doctor said she has to drink it or she'll be back in the hospital."

My dad said nothing.

"She's down to sixty-five pounds. Say something, dammit."

"Let me talk to her," I said, emerging from my bedroom.

My father started to yell at me. "Stay out of this."

"I'm her sister!"

"I told you, stay out of this!"

Mom was crying now. "Go to Jamie's house."

So I went to Jamie's house and she was watching The Skipper yell at Gilligan. I turned her TV off.

Jamie turned to me. "What are you doing?"

"They're taking my sister to the hospital."

"What happened?"

I told her about my morning.

That was three months ago. Now my mother's yelling again. She's screaming and I'm writing again, where I want to be, where I am in my head all the time. I'm writing as fast as I possibly can before I'm forced to have the welcome home family dinner.

In California at the beach, the brown surfer boy is waiting for me. My hair is streaked and my skin is tan from the sun; there is permanent salt on my skin that he loves to lick.

"Lilly!"

"Just a minute, Mom!"

My nose is peeled and a tattoo shows below my belly. There's a long-haired bearded man on the beach who sells burritos and fresh fruit smoothies. He is happy and we see him everyday, his five-year-old daughter in cutoff jeans playing in the sand at his side. One day it's so hot the surfer boy and I go to the mountains and there is snow. We roll in it and laugh our heads off. We are...

"Lilly!"

"One minute!"

"No! Get in here now! Your sister will be home soon! It's been three months, and it would be nice if she came back to a room without all your clothes thrown on the floor! Remember, she is in a fragile state!"

Can't finish, Jess is coming home. I'm NOT going to clean my room and act all sweet for her homecoming, my anorexic sister who just got out of the hospital. Mom got a welcome home chocolate cake, like Jess would eat it. No frigin' way. They are all insane.

I shut my diary. Walking down the narrow hallway to the kitchen, the ugly but soft beige wall-to-wall carpet at my feet, I yelled to my mom, "I'll be back in ten minutes. I'm going to the store."

I ran out fast down the driveway of our 1950s-style ranch house, which I hated; see, there are two other ones next door that look exactly like ours. I tried to ignore Mom who was yelling my name. Stopping and turning, I got the lie ready in my head.

"Mom, I'll be five minutes. I have to get something for Jessie that I forgot. She'll like it. Then I'll clean my room."

Mom backed down and went inside. Once upon a time, I wished she would insist, be stricter for once. Punish me. Things were far beyond that now.

I walked to the trolley station that was two streets over by the huge houses of Crystal Lake. I climbed down the woody embankment and onto the part of track past the station stop where people waited for the trolley.

I loved to walk on train tracks. It started in the sixth grade four years ago whenever my parents were fighting, which was all the time. I saw the wide, open tracks as a way to clear my head and be by myself. The tracks didn't have a third rail, like the tracks in other cities. They had above rails that were electric. I didn't know how they worked; I just knew a train could hit me but not electrocute me. So I would dodge them.

I wanted a black licorice stick at George's Folly, but now there was no time. George's Folly was all the way in Brookline, and I lived in Newton. Walking it was forty minutes at least. I just needed to clear my head before Jess got home.

It was the end of May and Jessie was supposed to graduate high school with honors and go to B.U. in September. Now she had missed three months and was coming home from the hospital. Who knew what would happen.

I put my hands in my pockets and felt a big hole in the right one. I cut these old Levi jeans so short that it was like they were only pockets, no legs.

It was warm out and my legs were getting tan already, the kind of brown that surfer girls have. I loved to get tan.

I had on my favorite tee shirt from a club on Martha's Vineyard that a girl named Claire gave me last summer. It was red and tight with a dog on it and "Bogart's bar" in faded white letters. What a great time Jamie, Beth, and I had, camping out, swimming, and meeting new people. Maybe we would go again this summer.

In my other pocket, I found the small spiral notebook I had been looking for. I opened it. There were my notes.

"Make Jamie rope bracelet for her birthday." The second page was the start of a poem about the boy with the pink sneakers from Cambridge.

"Far off eyes, where have you been, can I go too?"

The third page was the start of a drawing, a girl with long hair, wide eyes, rich thick lips, and a pug nose.

There was a pebble in my sneaker. They were dirty white Converses with all my friends' signatures on them and other pictures I had drawn in boring classes.

"Watch it!"

I jumped. The voice came from a hobo who was lying about twenty yards from me on the left side of the track. Was he dangerous? I walked slowly past him. He looked harmless. No knives or anything that I could see. Usually hobos aren't violent. Maybe he was just a homeless guy hanging out on the tracks. He was white, had a beard, and had dirt everywhere on his face, in his ears, and in his mangled hair.

"Watch what?"

"The rain. In thirty minutes, just you wait."

A train was coming around the corner. We both watched it before responding, me stepping off to the other side and the hobo rolling over to the edge.

The light was dimming, and I knew time was running out. I started to walk faster, looking down at the track as the train went by.

"Hey, you have any money?"

I reached in my pocket to find some change. I walked back a few steps and tossed the money near him, glancing at his legs, which were cut off at the knees with his pants hanging loose. There was a battered wheelchair off to the side in the bushes.

"What's your hurry?"

I started walking and for some reason said, "My sister's getting out of the hospital, and I need to get home."

"Good luck. And watch out for the rain."

I started walking. "Thanks."

"Come back again soon."

I wanted to tell him that it was MY stretch of track but instead said, "Sure."

The sky was getting dark, and I knew it was time to turn around. I had a knot in my stomach. I thought walking would help, so I continued onward.

My thoughts turned to Jess. Before she went away, my parents had been walking on tiptoes around her. They bent themselves into pretzels so she wouldn't get upset. Then when she lost more weight and got down to the dreaded sixty-five pounds, she had to go to the eating disorder unit. And now she was coming home, everyone hoping she was cured. I missed her and wondered how she had changed.

I was passing Crystal Lake on my left. There was a path on the right up to the street. There was a huge boulder right before the path, and three boys were sitting there. I stopped and they looked up. They looked vaguely familiar from Newton North High School; I went to Newton South. One had long, dirty blond hair, was skinny, and had no shirt on. His chest and belly were clear and smooth. One had dark black skin and an Afro and wore round glasses, and the third was a cute white guy who I recognized. He also had a black Afro.

"Hey, sexy girl, come get high with us," the shirtless guy called.

I smelled the sweet smoke from reefer.

I didn't know if I should stop, but the whole thing looked too inviting.

Shirtless guy said, "It's OK. We won't bite."

White Afro kid said, "I will."

I walked up to them and leaned on a tree, knowing that I should be home.

They introduced themselves. Billy (shirtless), Joey (white Afro, cute), and Darryl (black, handsome, glasses, Afro). They passed the joint to me. I took a few deep tokes and felt a familiar buzz. My whole body relaxed.

Joey looked at me really closely. "I know you, sexy girl." He had these really big brown eyes with long black lashes. When he looked at me, I felt kissed. He was so cute, with dimples, full lips, and a sneaky smile.

He slanted his head and smiled at me.

"Do you want to come to California with me? I'm going this summer."

I looked over at the lake. It had sparkles of the setting sun, and now I was officially stoned, feeling the relaxation and heaviness of good reefer.

The first time I got high on weed I was so freaked out; the walls in Debbie's house were melting and everything sounded like an echo. Debbie called Harry, the guy who got me the reefer. Debbie was too scared to do any so it was just me. Harry told me to suck a lemon, which I did, and somehow it helped. After that, I was used to it and liked it so much. Debbie stopped hanging out with me. I missed her but she was so goody-goody and only wanted to watch soap operas. Mostly I missed her mother who was nice to me and let me eat all the peanut butter cookies and her sister Joni who would let me go in her room and look at her music collection and would talk with me about anything in the world.

I took another long toke and looked into Joey's eyes. I fell in love with him in an instant.

"Yes, I do want to go to California with you, but my sister is coming home from the hospital so I have to be home…umm…half an hour ago."

Joey reached over and touched my hair. It was shoulder-length, brown, with natural red and blond streaks, and soft as silk.

"Wow, your hair is soft."

Billy jumped up. "Let me feel it. I love soft hair. I have soft hair too, feel it." He reached for the other side of my hair and gave me a chunk of his hair to feel.

We all sat there doing the hair-feeling thing. A breeze came up that had a late-May coolness to it. The stars were starting to come out. Despite the reefer and the company, I knew I was so late. I really didn't want trouble, not tonight, and I could sense my mother's anxiety wafting toward the lake.

One more toke and I got up. "I really got to go."

Joey stood up also. "I'll walk you home."

I didn't want anyone walking near my crazy house. It looked normal from the outside, except in my recurring nightmare where it changes shape as the man with the axe chases me around the house.

"No, it's OK, I'm good."

Joey came up behind me and put his arms around my shoulders. I turned and he gave me a soft, sexy kiss on my lips. I giggled and smiled.

I will never leave now, was my thought. I breathed in his scent, something woodsy.

"Meet us in Cambridge tonight. There's a concert at the Common." Joey was holding on to my hand. I let it go and ran up the path to the sidewalk.

"Bye sexy girl," Billy called out.

I was smiling the first few minutes walking, but then the butterflies came back. What if Dad was home already? Would their need for a perfect homecoming bring out the big weapons? The tongue-lashing, the alligator belt maybe?

I started running, the knots in my stomach mixing with flyaway thoughts. It started to rain lightly. Just like the hobo had said.

Come on, darkness, fly me home. What will Jessie be like? Why didn't they let me visit? She's my sister, I missed her, and they didn't let me visit her for three months. What was that? Did you miss me, Jessie? Let me in on the secrets. Mom worried every second, and Dad stopped talking completely, except to shout, so it was the crazy people and me.

What if I never made it home…just kept going…and going… going?

CHAPTER TWO

Homecoming

I ran into the kitchen and found my mom stirring something on the stove, a glass of red wine on the counter.
I read her face and saw that she wouldn't yell at me; she
was sad and drinking her second glass at least.

"Is she here yet?"

She spoke softly. "Yes, she came in twenty minutes ago.
It would have been nice if you had been here. But don't
bother her; she's resting in her bedroom."

Which is my bedroom too.

"I'm going to talk to her." I walked out of the kitchen.

"Lilly!"

I turned. "What?"

"Don't mention the hospital."

I shook my head and walked down the hall. Don't
mention the hospital. Jess has been gone for three months
to a hospital for girls who starve themselves, and I should
pretend she's been on a cruise.

I opened the door to our room. Jessie was on her bed
reading a book.

"Hey!" I bounced over to her and gave her a big hug. I felt Jessie's bones under her loose clothes.

"Hi!" Jessie smiled and seemed genuinely glad to see me. "What's up?"

I sat on the floor between our beds, leaning against mine. "What's up with you? How was the hospital?"

Our room was small with two identical single beds side by side and a table in between. We had identical headboards, identical desks, and purple wall-to-wall carpet. The curtains were heavy purple with big, purple square patterns. Mom picked the colors. We put up posters; the walls were full of them. Jimi Hendrix with his guitar, a Beatles poster, a poster that said "War is not healthy for children and other living things" with two beautiful children holding hands, a huge peace symbol in rainbow colors, and a poster left over from our ballet days, Degas' dancers.

"It was awful. They forced everyone to eat and went to the bathroom with you to make sure you didn't puke. Can't you tell?" She spread out her arms. "I gained about one hundred pounds."

I stared at her. "You look great."

"I want to show you the pictures I drew while I was there. It will explain what happened. A pictorial."

Jessie reached under her bed and came out with a leather bound book. I sat next to her.

"I'm so glad you're home! You know baseball season started, so Mom and Dad have been fighting so much. Dad's been watching the games and betting. He has a long business trip in July, which Mom was screaming about. Same old same old."

"Look at these pictures."

The first picture was of a building with bars on the windows.

Jessie started narrating in a soft voice. "OK, the journey starts with the building. See this window? The third floor. That's where all the pretty starving girls were."

I looked at her closely. She was way too calm. "Are you on drugs?"

Jessie laughed. "Yeah, the happy pills. I made them promise I wouldn't gain weight on them. Here, this was my best friend."

The picture Jessie drew was of a pretty blond girl with a skeleton body. "She was even thinner than me. She was on IV so she wouldn't die."

I watched Jess turn the pages and show me drawings of girls, all with skeleton bodies, but with different pretty faces.

"What happened to them? I mean, are they still there?"

Jessie looked dreamily at the pages. "Some. A few got out this week too."

I was amazed at my sister's talent to draw and at all the skinny girls in the pictures.

"That's crazy, I mean, all those girls. Was it fun at all?" I got up and looked for music to put on our record player. We had Grateful Dead, Beatles, Allman Brothers, J. Geils, Bonnie Raitt, Jimi Hendrix, Jim Morrison, and Marvin Gaye. I picked out the Dead. Joey, the white Afro boy I just met, looked a little like Jerry Garcia, the lead guitar player.

Jessie lay back on her pillow. "No, Lilly, it wasn't fun. It was like prison."

I sat back down on the floor holding the album cover. "Jess, I just met these guys from Newton North. Billy, Joey, Darryl. Maybe you know them?"

Jessie flipped through the pages of her book. "I don't know. What about them? Look, here's a picture of my shrink. He was gorgeous. I get to see him twice a week."

"Mom should go."

"Yeah, she won't. They came once and wouldn't say anything. Mom just cried and Dad looked mad. Why didn't you come?"

"I wanted to! They wouldn't let me."

"Oh." Jessie stared at her pictures.

"Look, Jess." I gave her the album cover and pointed to Jerry Garcia, with his bushy black hair. "Joey looks like this, except no beard. He's so cute. I want to go with him to California, and Jess, you have to help me figure out how. You're so smart."

"Dinner's ready!" Mom opened the door and looked at us on the bed together.

"It's nice to see you girls talking," she said and looked sharply at me.

"What?" I hated trying to read what my mom was thinking since she never said it outright.

We all sat down at the dinner table, Dad at the head and Mom scurrying around getting all the food on the table. Barbecued chicken, roasted potatoes, salad, and mixed vegetables.

I was starving, which happens after smoking pot, so I piled tons of food on my plate.

"Take a little at a time, Lilly!" Mom said.

"I'm hungry."

Jessie's plate had normal amounts on it. My parents tried to talk about things like the weather and work, but they were sneaking glances at Jessie the whole time.

"Stop watching me eat!" Jessie burst into tears and ran from the table to our room, slamming the door.

Mom stood up. "You were watching her too much. The doctor said to just let it alone."

Dad yelled, "I didn't look once! You're the one tiptoeing around her."

Mom went after her and Dad turned on the small television we weren't supposed to watch at dinner. We ate watching the news. I didn't care. I ate three pieces of chicken and four helpings of potatoes; the chocolate cake never made it to the table, so I cut a chunk and stuffed it in my mouth. I cleared my plate and went back to my room to get ready to go out. I wondered if they would make me stay in with Jess. It was Saturday night and I usually went out. I wanted to go find the guys in Cambridge.

In the room Jessie was drawing, nibbling on some crackers she had stored under her bed. I guessed my mom was in her room. My parents had separate bedrooms, although one was supposed to be an office.

"Can you go out yet? I'm going to Cambridge; some bands are playing on the Common. Come with me."

Jessie kept drawing, not looking up. "I'm tired."

I grabbed my favorite jacket, brown leather with fringe, and decided to keep on my shorts and tee. I passed the kitchen on my way out and saw Mom cleaning up. She was crying.

"Mom, what's wrong?"

"Your father. He's downstairs watching TV and not helping with Jessie one bit."

I went over to her. "Mom, Jess is all right. She's just drawing. Don't worry, Mom, she'll be OK."

I stroked her hair. "I'm just going to Jamie's house; I'll be back by ten. Don't be sad, Mom, it will all work out."

"I wish I could go out. Your father never takes me anywhere."

"Sometime you can come out with me. But I don't know if you'd have fun with my friends. Maybe just you and I can go out sometime."

Her eyes lit up. "That would be nice, Lilly."

I kissed her on the cheek and snuck past my Dad, quietly locking the door behind me.

On Centre Street, I stuck out my thumb. That familiar panicky feeling hit my chest. Or was it excitement? Never knowing who was going to stop. I had refused rides before if the people looked too creepy. I mean, I wasn't stupid.

A car pulled over. I ran up to the door and saw two hippies in the front, tie-dyed, long hair, smiling. Relieved, I climbed in the back. The guy was Mitch and the girl Valerie, and they were nice hippies going all the way to Cambridge.

I looked out the window. The woman was chattering away, and then turned to me.

"We could use a babysitter for our three-year-old girl, Flower. Do you want a job?"

"Yeah, sure. But I'm going to California with my boyfriend soon." Somehow that was funny to her, and she laughed loudly as Mitch lit a joint. I watched as we went onto Storrow Drive. After going across the bridge over the Charles River, we were in Harvard Square.

They let me out in front of The Coop. Valerie gave me a joint, and I was on the sidewalk, breathing in the cool night air. I heard music coming from Cambridge Common. Just where I wanted to be. I ran past the ancient graveyard and crossed the street into the pearly gates of Cambridge Common, my most favorite place on earth.

CHAPTER THREE

Virginity

People were everywhere. They were dancing, lying on blankets, all facing this enormous bandstand. The sweet smell of marijuana filled the air. I walked into the crowd.

Someone grabbed my arm. "Hey, sexy girl!" It was Billy from the lake.

He was standing next to Joey.

"Sexy girl!" Joey gave me a big kiss on the lips.

The girl behind him screamed. "Lilly!" It was Jamie, who was hanging with Joey and Billy. She went to Newton North too, but I didn't know she knew them.

The band was playing "Purple Haze" by Jimi Hendrix. Someone passed me a joint and a bottle of wine at the same time. I gave back the wine and took a deep toke of the joint. Then Joey grabbed me from behind and squeezed me, dancing.

"Hey, want to trip?"

I thought he was talking about his trip so I yelled back, "Yeah I want to go!"

He gave me a blot of paper. There was a drawing of a peach on it.

"Only take half, it's strong!"

Before I put it in my mouth I asked, "What am I eating?"

"LSD. Acid. Eat a Peach. Just half, for a little buzz. Won't be more than a flying high. I LOVE the stuff! Pure, no bad trips, guaranteed!"

I felt excited and scared. I had done a small amount of acid before and had fun, seeing walls melt and people's faces change. As long as I didn't have to go home. I would tell my parents I was sleeping at Jamie's.

We swayed to the music. During the guitar solo, Joey whispered in my ear, "Come to California with me."

"Yes, yes, yes!" I screamed and we danced. The music was blasting in my ears, making them buzz, the air smelled sweet, and I felt far away from my house in Newton.

After a while of dancing, I stopped and backed off the crowd to look. Colors flashed before my eyes like a rainbow. I felt strong and really tall.

Jamie danced over to me. She was clear-eyed. "Are you tripping?"

Her face looked like a painting. I nodded.

"Are you?"

She shook her head. "Not tonight. But you can stay at my house with everyone else! My step-bitch is away with my dad. Come on, we're all going now and we can call your house walking to the subway."

We found a pay phone. I stopped laughing long enough to tell my mom that I was staying at Jamie's. It was OK with her, as long as I was back tomorrow to be with 'the family', which would consist of my dad watching sports, Mom complaining, and the good part, my sister and I hanging out in our room making up games and listening to music.

"Your mom is naïve," Jamie said when we were seated in the subway.

"No, it's wine."

"Your eyes are dilating so much!"

It sounded like an echo and her mouth looked huge. All I could do was laugh and hide my eyes at the very bright subway lights.

Everyone was sitting in a row: Darryl, Beth and her boyfriend Ted, Jamie, Kate, Billy, Joey, and a few boys I didn't know.

Joey put his head on my belly and started biting under my tee shirt.

"Stop!" I giggled and looked up at a white-haired man staring. He looked super mean like he was gonna stab my belly. I held tighter on to Joey's arm.

Beth came over to sit next to me. She was my sister's age, a senior, and had her classes in another part of Newton South. I hugged her even though she looked mean too.

"When did you get together with Joey and why didn't you tell me?"

I whispered, "It just happened. Today."

Her mouth, like a huge fish, opened and closed. I think she laughed.

"Lilly, you have to tell me these details, I don't like surprises!" She stormed away or did she slink? Was she laughing or mad? Did she like him too? The thoughts went in and out like a thundercloud with no rain.

I leaned against Joey, closed my eyes, and watched the colors float by in my brain.

We are on a train ride forever. A road trip with wheat fields.

We got to Jamie's house around midnight. Her father was a lawyer and they lived in one of the large Tudor houses off Beacon Street.

In the house Jamie put on some music and brought out tons of snacks. Everyone was starving. I tried to eat, but it all tasted like cardboard. I was so stoned on the acid; everything was slow motion. The music was even on low speed, but it wasn't.

Joey took my hand and led me to a room off the living room. He closed the door, but we could still hear everyone talking and the music playing.

"Lie down with me, sexy girl."

"OK, sexy boy," I meant to say, but it came out like "OK, cowboy" and disappeared. I was peaking on the acid and feeling like I was in a tunnel. I kept hearing echoes that smelled like flowers, making everything feel like a movie. It was curious, not unpleasant, and not totally comfortable. I thought everyone was here and then I looked around and it was only Joey, lying next to me on the bed. He took off his shirt and his body looked neon. His heart sounded like thunder. I ran my fingers over his chest. It was so soft. He put his arms around me, and I never felt anything better in my life. We kissed and it was like dew drops. Kissing and licking, touching, laughing. It was a heavenly rainstorm.

We lay side by side. His body was warm as it rubbed against me. Everything felt slow.

He was breathing hard as I felt him taking off his pants. I thought to be afraid but I wasn't.

"You a virgin?" he whispered. His mouth looked like a guppy, the words garbled.

I laughed and he said, "Never mind. I'll find out."

He moved on top of me, taking something out of his back pocket and ripping it open. I thought he was giving me some candy, maybe a red hot, which I wanted.

"I want a red hot."

"Yeah I have a red hot."

He pressed against my body and it felt like a hot, hard snake landed on me.

I screamed and rolled off the bed. "What was that?"

Jamie came running in and when she saw Joey naked and me on the floor, she started to laugh.

"Shut up! We're good! Now get out!" Joey pointed to the door.

She stood her ground. "It's MY house. Lilly, you OK?"

The dark floor with the carpet had movement like a carnival ride.

"Totally," I managed to say. I saw the words trail out of my mouth, hanging onto Jamie's long, blond hair as she closed the door.

Joey came down to join the ride. We rolled together on the floor.

"I want to have sex with you," he said, lying on top of me, his breathing heavy.

It was hard to understand, the words were echoes and colors.

"Just be nice," I said.

Joey took off my shorts. He was warm against me and then in me. It felt like a pushing and then he let out a big sound. That part of my body felt tingling and then it went down to my toes. Which felt like they were huge.

My hand caught my attention then. I could see all the veins popping out in green and yellow. Joey grabbed it and I said, "Careful of the insides." He pulled me up to the bed and snuggled his body toward mine. I was still looking at the hand, wondering how it got to be invisible. Joey kissed me yummy on the lips and curled himself around me.

Hours must have gone by as he slept and I went in and out of dream and live visions. And then it was light out again.

I was alone in the bed. The table clock said two. At night? In the day? Was that possible? My thoughts were squeezing through this tiny hole in my brain. I didn't understand it. Then I remembered that I did Eat a Peach acid last night.

I had slept with Joey and now he wasn't there. We may have had sex, which would be my first time. There were no signs, no blood on the bed, nothing.

I went looking for him and found him in Jamie's kitchen leaning against the fridge eating out of a box of Frosted Flakes. I went over to him and he kissed me. His crunching was making scratches on my brain, and my head felt like a bowling ball. Acid hangovers.

I wanted to ask him if we had sex but felt like it would be weird if I didn't remember. So I asked if he used protection, and he smiled, said yes, and gave me a kiss. So. I was no longer a virgin. Too bad I didn't remember anything about it.

I opened the refrigerator. Basic groceries—eggs, milk, cold cuts, parent-looking food in containers. I opened the freezer. That was more like it. Friendly's chocolate chip ice cream, a whole gallon. Joey and I looked at each other and smiled.

Billy came in, shirtless, his long stringy hair in his face. Joey and I had spoons and were in heaven, the cold sweet ice cream doing the trick. Wordlessly Billy got a spoon and stood eating with us, as Jamie, Ted, Beth, and Darryl filed in.

"What's happening!" Darryl put his arms out to all of us.

Everyone raided Jamie's kitchen. I stood there with the same buzz and the same good feeling with Joey's arm around me. He didn't wander to Kate or Beth or the long red-haired singer whose name I forgot. He stayed by my side. Smelling my hair. Touching it. Intertwining his fingers in me. Pulling my arm, leading me back to the room, having another kiss and another feel and another, this time it was easier and nicer, and I wanted to go to California right then, not finish tenth grade, not go back to my family, just start the adventure.

We fell asleep again and when I woke up Joey was talking to Billy who was sitting on the chair next to our bed.

"Two days after school ends, June 28, Lilly and I are out of here. Heading west! Barry, my older brother is driving us. You should come! No parents, nothing. It will be a blast." The conversation went on and on and I wondered about the time. It felt like days since I had been home and the butterflies were starting through the haze in my brain from the acid.

Ted had a car and offered me a ride to Newton Centre. Joey gave me a huge kiss and I left with Ted. He dropped me off at the church and that's when I freaked out; the church clock said seven. Maybe it was broken? Where had the day gone? Had I called my parents? I didn't remember much as I ran the rest of the way home, feeling that familiar panic when I turned into my street. I wondered when I was going to see Joey again and felt that pull and yearning, the empty ache like maybe that was the whole thing, last night, yesterday.

Sunday nights at my house were all about sports and my parents' fighting. Dad had the two TVs set up to watch Red Sox and some golf game. I slipped by him to go upstairs, or so I thought.

"Lilly!"

I walked back down the stairs.

"Hi, Dad."

He walked over to me and smelled my hair. "You've been smoking."

"No, Dad. A kid who was at Jamie's smokes. Not me, though." I smiled as close to an innocent smile as I could muster.

He shook his head. "If I ever catch you hitchhiking…"

"Hitchhiking? Who ever said anything about hitchhiking? Do you think I'm crazy? You can get killed hitchhiking, Dad." I didn't smile; I looked down instead.

By now the conversation was over because Arnold Palmer or someone was putting and Carlton Fisk was up.

Our room was at the end of the hall across from my parents' room, so close you could hear a sneeze, a cough, a teardrop.

My mom was in bed watching *All in the Family*.

"Hi Mom, I'm home. I'm tired and going to bed."

She looked at me and said I was grounded for three nights for being late. Seeing as it was Sunday and the next three days were school nights, I didn't care. But I pretended I did.

Jessie was in her bed reading. She had homework to catch up on. She was a straight-A student and worried about what she missed so was doing double time.

I plopped down on my bed and turned to Jessie.

"I am so tired. I barely slept. But I had fun! We were at Jamie's and Joey was there! He's my new boyfriend; you have to meet him. There's a whole crowd of kids; you can go with me next time."

Jessie looked pale and sad. "I don't feel that much like going out right now, Lilly."

She stuck her nose back in her book.

I remembered something. "Hey Jessie, I wrote you a poem while you were away. Well, not really for you but… about you."

She put her book down. "Let me hear it."

I went into my drawer that was next to her drawer and pulled out a crumbled piece of paper.

"It's called "Broken Heart."

Jessie barely lifted her head from the pillow.

"You OK?"

"Yeah. Just really tired."

I wondered if she had eaten, if she was going to break down again.

"Read it to me."

"OK. Don't laugh or be mad."

"No."

I started softly. "*Broken Heart*" by Me."

"When you left I looked for you.
Under the bed, in the closet, maybe in the playroom, I thought.
I looked in the usual places.
Watching television, doing your homework.
Everything was empty when you left.
You left me, now my heart is broken.
Our dolls are crying and so am I. When are you coming back?"

I turned to Jessie. "I didn't finish it."

"It's really depressing." She picked up her book.

"Yeah well it was really depressing around here. Please get better so you don't leave again. They were so awful. The fights were so bad."

Jessie lifted her head and said, "You probably didn't stay around much anyway to notice."

"Yeah, well, enough. Anyway, Joey and I are going to California this summer. In one month."

"How are you going to swing that?"

"When school gets out. I'm gonna ask if I can go with his family. Like, pretend his whole family is going. Only it's just me and him and his older brother who drives. VW bus. The whole thing."

"Dad will never let you."

"Maybe he will. He doesn't seem to care about anything anymore, since, well…you know." I turned my head away.

"Since I got sick. Since I went into the hospital."

"Everything got messed up."

"Well don't blame me! They said not to blame yourself because it's an illness. Part of it is being perfect. So don't blame me!"

"It's true that they were fighting long before you got sick."

I took off my clothes and looked in the mirror. I was OK with my body; my legs were long and my stomach was flat. My boobs were OK too.

"I need a tan."

I put on my sweatpants and a tee shirt and climbed in bed.

Jessie put her book carefully on the carpet next to her bed. "Can we turn off the light now?"

We turned off the light and I stared at the ceiling. The streetlights were flicking, looking like Tinkerbelle. Maybe I was still tripping.

"Jess?"

"Umm?"

"How was it away? I mean, did you like getting away from here for a while?"

There was silence for a minute. Then Jessie said, "Yeah, it was peaceful. Everyone was telling their secrets."

"That's pretty cool."

"Yeah, it was."

I listened to her breathing, glad she was home.

"Night, Jess."

"Night, Lilly."

A place where secrets were told and everyone has them. A road trip to somewhere else. A road trip where secrets are told, or kept, or made. I couldn't wait.

CHAPTER FOUR

Road Trip

Barry was eating a box of Captain Crunch cereal sitting in a big leather chair in his den. Joey and I were sitting across from him in another huge chair, me on Joey's lap. I had a chocolate Tootsie Roll Pop and he was eating a frozen Sarah Lee pound cake.

Barry wiped off cereal crumbs on his Mickey Mouse tee shirt. "So, we'll leave on the twenty-eighth. We're going south first, to UNC in Raleigh. I have a friend there. The first long stop will be in New Mexico. If you kids want to stop somewhere special, let me know, and I'll put it on the itinerary."

"Austin!" Joey spit dry cold pound cake all over my arm.

"Gross! Close your mouth! And how can you eat that frozen?"

He smiled and all the cake squeezed out of his teeth. I looked away. Was he trying to be disgusting?

"The cake melts when it hits your tongue. Here, try some."

"I'll pass. So Barry, are we going all the way to California?"

"That's the plan." Barry was nineteen, had been in college for a year, and was on the lookout for another college to transfer to.

Joey looked a little like Barry except Barry had a beard and mustache and was heavier, not fat but hefty. He seemed nice enough, seemed like I could hang with him for a road trip.

"We did great convincing Lilly's parents that it was cool for her to go and that our parents were going too. I was good at playing Dad. No offense, Lilly, but your mom is really gullible. She said you have to be back in six weeks to go to your beach house. I told her there would be another girl and that Joey is just a school friend, so you," he pointed at Joey, "need to stay away from her house until we get back."

"No problem. Anything you say. You are the man. I am so happy Lilly can go; I'll do anything you say. We are going to rock and roll!" Joey let out a holler and reached over to his guitar. I sat next to him and he started strumming.

"You also need to cool it on the excessive drugging and drinking, especially on the road. I'm not taking care of you again."

Joey began tuning his guitar. "Bro, that was only once. Or twice. I'll be good."

I put my fingers in his Afro and pulled a little. He looked up at me.

"Joey, are you a drug addict or alchie? You better tell me now."

He tried to take the lollipop out of my mouth, so I cracked it and chewed the whole thing in a few bites and he got the stick.

"Course not. I'm only seventeen! And, I'll wear my favorite cross; it will protect me." He pulled out a chain he was wearing around his neck. It was a gold cross with a small diamond in it.

I was confused. "I thought you were Jewish."

Joey put the necklace back in his shirt. "I am. I just like crosses."

Barry shook his head. "Mom would have a heart attack if she saw that thing."

Joey started playing a Dead song and singing, "Sugar Magnolia, blossoms blooming, heads all empty and I don't care, saw my baby down by the river, knew she'd have to come up soon for air."

It sounded pretty good. "That's cool! You should bring your guitar on the road trip."

Barry got up from his chair. "Don't encourage him. That's the only song he knows." He walked over to a huge entertainment system with Bose speakers, a very large television, receivers, amps, and a bunch of other equipment. Joey and Barry's parents had loads of money. Their house was humongous with many rooms and a full-time maid, cook, and driver. Their parents would be in Europe all summer, except the last few weeks when they would all meet at their Martha's Vineyard compound. That's what Joey called it. He had said to me, "When we get back from our road trip, you'll have to come with me to the compound. It's a blast."

Barry turned on the television. "I'm serious about the drugs, Joey. I will leave you in the middle of a cornfield if you mess up!"

Joey strummed his guitar strings harder. I wondered if he was mad, but when I looked at him he smiled. "No problem, bro, I'll behave."

"So leaving day is the twenty-eighth. Now get out of here so I can watch *M*A*S*H*."

Joey put his guitar down and pulled me off the chair. We walked outside to meet our friends at the Newton Centre Brigham's. The whole time walking we talked about the trip. I was so excited, I wanted to skip the last month of school and leave right away.

The last few weeks of school went by so slowly. Jessie stayed home and read, doing her exams from the house. I managed to finish most of my work and stayed focused on the road trip.

Finally school was over and it was June 27, the day before the trip. When I woke up I went to the train tracks to walk to Newton Centre and meet my friends.

What I loved about walking on train tracks was the solitude. Hardly anyone was ever there and it helped me think. Also I loved the danger. Not knowing when the trains were coming, seeing them from afar, getting out of the way. Watching them pass, wondering about the people inside, who they were and where they were coming from, where they were going.

I saw my hobo friend a few minutes after I started. He was further down the line this time by Newton Centre. He was sitting by the side smoking a cigar—a big fat cigar like the old guys smoked. It looked like he had taken a bath; his hands were clean, except for the nails. I came on him by surprise, and I must have jumped because he laughed.

"I don't bite, my friend."

Then he asked about my sister.

"You have a good memory. She's OK, I don't really know."

"Are you planning your big escape?"

At this point my mouth dropped open and I stared hard. Then I shook my head. "No. No big escape."

He smiled in a way that told me he absolutely did not believe me.

"OK. Just make sure you say good-bye before you go."

I walked away, fast. I looked back once and he was smiling at me. Not creepy, just knowing. Who was this man?

I was meeting Kate, Beth, and Jamie at Brigham's to say good-bye. We were all going to meet at my beach house in August to compare summer notes. Kate was going to Maine with her family, Beth was a counselor at a summer camp, and Jamie went to the Cape with her family.

When I got there, Beth was with Ted. He was totally baked on downers and Beth was playing nurse. She was trying to keep him on the counter stool. The manager kicked us out after Ted's head fell into his coffee cup and it broke in a million pieces. We took him outside and walked him around. Thankfully Billy drove up and we put him in his car to be driven home. Beth and Kate went with them, and that was the end of our farewell ice cream. I hugged Jamie and we promised we'd meet at my beach house.

I walked home quickly because I was late, as usual. I was trying to be a 'good girl' so they wouldn't take away my road trip. I was amazed they were letting me go. I think it was that they were so concerned with Jessie getting better, and I was one less kid to deal with. Out of sight, out of mind, I guess. And my dad was travelling all of July on business, which was cause for the last eighty fights.

At home I said hello to my mom and went to my room. Jessie was asleep on her bed.

I got a duffle bag from my closet and took out my list. I put things in one at a time.

LIST OF THINGS TO BRING:

2 blank books (big ones without lines so I can draw)
2 pairs of jeans
2 pairs of jean shorts
4 tee shirts
2 sweatshirts
3 sundresses
2 miniskirts
3 halter- tops
2 bikinis
Flip-flops
High tops
Frye boots (to wear the first day with my mini jean skirt and flowered halter top)
2 bras and 4 pairs of underwear (I could wash them? Or not wear any)
Books (On the Road, by Jack Kerouac The Prophet by Kahlil Gibran and The Hobbit)
Indian fringe pocketbook
Wallet, brush, and toothbrush/ toothpaste
Credit card (Mom gave me in case of emergency; Dad doesn't know!)

"You're not actually going, are you?" Jessie's eyes were open and she was watching me.

I looked at her to determine the meaning of the question. I couldn't read her face since her long hair was covering her expression.

"Yes, I'm actually going. What's that supposed to mean?"

"Nothing. I just thought you might not want to leave me here alone, especially since I just got back from the hospital."

Wow. Who would have thought she would go down this road. I stopped packing.

"What are you talking about?"

She picked up a book, Carlos Castaneda. "Nothing. Never mind."

"Jessie, what?"

"Nothing. It's just that, without you here getting in trouble every two minutes, they're going to watch me. And you know how that is."

"Maybe they won't. You know, since you went to the hospital, they don't want to…upset you."

She put the book down and glanced at my duffle bag. I was putting the books in and trying to close it.

She got up and helped me push everything down and then tie it. "Yeah. Maybe."

I suddenly felt the urge to hug her, so I did. Real tight. I felt her bones.

"Don't crush me!" she pulled away and laughed.

"Look, if it gets bad, meet me on the road somewhere."

Jessie nodded and lay back down on her bed. I knew she wouldn't ever join me. She couldn't do a thing that would possibly upset Mom. I felt bad for her, and I also felt like I wanted to leave fast, just to stop the other feeling that was burning a hole in my feet.

That was our good-bye because when I left early the next morning, she was asleep. My dad was at work so we didn't get to say good-bye either, and my mom was walking circles around the kitchen, smoking one of her five Winston cigarettes she let herself have a day. She had a strong cup of tea in front of her.

"Mom, my ride is outside, I gotta go." I had my duffle bag over my shoulder.

"Call me if you need anything," she said, vaguely.

"I will, Mom. I'll call a lot to check in and talk with Jessie too. I love you."

I kissed her on the cheek. She looked like she was still in a dream so I didn't say anything else. Neither did she; maybe she would have said, "Let me meet everyone before you go," or, "Be safe," or "I changed my mind, there's no way you are going."

The Volkswagen bus turned out to be a bright yellow 1974 Volkswagen Bug. It was a good thing there was only three of us. I stuck my duffle bag in the back with their backpacks, camping gear, and a couple bags of food.

Barry was in the driver's seat. Joey turned around and gave me a big kiss on the lips.

"Ready for the best road trip of your life?" He screamed.

"Yes!"

Barry backed out of my driveway. I saw my mom by the curtain, peeking out. As we drove down the road to 95 South, I waved, to her, my house, my sister, to Newton, everything. I felt a wave of excitement, happiness, and a little something else deep inside that I couldn't place. Anyway, the radio was blasting Rolling Stones, and our road trip had begun!

CHAPTER FIVE

Snakes in North Carolina

We drank huge iced coffees with our favorite car food: Joey's was Oreo cookies, which he took all the insides out, made a huge ball of icing, and then ate that and then the cookie part; Barry's was sweet cereal like Fruit Loops or Captain Crunch, which he ate straight out of the box; and mine were Cheese Doodles and Tab soda, which had a gross aftertaste, but I liked anyway.

We hightailed it to North Carolina, with pit stops outside of New Haven, Philadelphia, and a lunch break outside of Richmond, Virginia. Then it was my turn to drive. Joey had been teaching me how to drive a stick shift in the parking lot of our high school for the past month. I thought I was pretty good at it, until I tried to merge onto the highway. I was stuck in third gear and couldn't go fast enough. Thank God the Mack Truck moved over to the middle lane. Finally, I was in fourth gear going sixty, the fastest the little bug would go. I didn't actually have a license yet since I was still fifteen, but I was a pretty good driver.

The windows were open, we were full of grilled cheese sandwiches and French fries, Bee Gees were playing, and the breeze was warm.

The song switched to country music and we settled in for the last stretch of the day to Chapel Hill. It was dusk and the light was beginning to dim. Barry had a friend who lived in Chapel Hill and went to the University. We were planning on staying with him for the night.

Ten minutes into driving, I had to pee so badly. I kept putting it off; one more exit, another, another.

"I really need to pee!" I yelled.

"So get off!" Barry was sitting next to me, reading a *Dennis the Menace* comic book.

"Which exit?" I looked around and everything was forest, no gas stations in sight.

He looked up briefly. "Any one."

I got off the next exit. Shifted into third, then second. Stopped at a cross street. Left or right? I went left and found myself on a country road. After ten minutes of driving through a forest, I realized I would have to use the woods. The country road turned to dirt, and after five more minutes, I found a spot to pull over.

Barry looked up. Joey woke up and said, "Where the hell are we?"

"I don't know. I have to pee!"

"Your girlfriend drove us into the boonies. Lilly, you better remember how to get back on the highway."

I ran into the woods and looked around. The only thing I saw was a cabin about one hundred yards from us. I went behind a tree, pulled up my skirt, and started to pee.

As the relief set in, I heard something rustle in the grass ahead of me. I saw something long, leathery, black and white, uncurling about ten feet ahead.

"Snake!" I screamed at the top of my lungs. Was I supposed to freeze or run? My skirt was bunched up around my waist, and I was squatting, unable to move.

"Snake!" I yelled again. Joey and Barry came running, Barry looking at a guidebook.

The snake was unwinding, moving slowly forward.

Barry whispered, "It's a timber rattlesnake. Can be dangerous. Snake handlers use them." He moved closer to me but kept his distance from the snake.

I whispered back, "I don't give a damn who uses them! Should I move?"

There was another rustling ahead of us in the direction of the cabin. A man with a shotgun was pointing it in our direction. Was he going to shoot us? We were trespassing on his land.

"Don't move."

Blast! He shot the snake, got it dead on, and it rolled over. I quickly adjusted my clothes and stood up as the man went over and nudged it with his very large black boots. He had on jeans and a flannel shirt, had long white hair and a scruffy face.

He bent down to look. "Dead." He picked it up and threw it over his shoulder. He turned, walking into the woods toward the cabin.

We were silent for a minute, stunned. Then I found my voice. "Thank you for saving my life!"

The man turned around slowly, as if deciding something.

"He wouldn't have hurt you." His voice sounded young, like a teenager. Looking closer he actually looked young, and I noticed that his hair was blond, not white.

Barry walked a few steps toward the man, holding his book out. "Is it a Timber Rattlesnake, particular to North Carolina, or could it be an Eastern Hognose snake?"

Joey laughed and Barry glared at him. "Shut up. It's good information to have."

"Timber rattlesnake, though not just from these parts." He turned to walk away and hesitated.

"You want to see something?"

Barry looked at Joey and me. I nodded vehemently. This guy with the dead snake over his shoulder interested me.

Joey said, "Sure," and we followed him to the cabin.

I took Joey's arm. "I hope he's not a murderer or something, with that big shotgun."

"I bet he has a lot more guns than that."

As we walked closer to the cabin I noticed that it was made with logs, just like the toy Lincoln Logs, with cut logs that fit into each other, insulation in between. The man held the door and we walked into a large room.

Barry let out a whistle. "You kill them all?"

The walls in his cabin were covered with snakeskins, all different types, colors, and sizes.

"Yep."

I walked close to the wall. There were neatly nailed snakeskins evenly spaced throughout the room. The room itself was very neat. It had a small, open kitchen in the back and a loft. There was a big wooden table with six chairs around it in the middle of the room. It was a one-room cabin. Joey was right, there were three shotguns over the fireplace by a huge pile of wood and a couple of axes.

There were some books on the table and no pictures anywhere. It was pretty bare bones.

Joey was walking around looking at the snakeskins. He said to the man, "Did you build this cabin?"

The man sat at the table and took out cigarette paper and tobacco. He rolled his own cigarette, took a match from behind his ear, and lit it on the sole of his boot.

"You want to sit for a minute?" He nodded to the chairs around him. Barry sat and Joey walked over too, pulling my arm and making me fall on top of him. I took my arm back and sat down.

On closer look at this man, he was really handsome. His hair was shoulder length and dirty blond, and his skin was tan. His eyes were a sky blue, so big and bright that it was like looking into the Caribbean Sea. He looked to be in his early twenties.

"Do you live here by yourself?"

He turned his head and looked at me deeply, like he was figuring out my whole life story. He puffed on his cigarette and nodded.

Barry pointed to walls. "Nice logs. You build it?"

"My granddad."

For some reason, maybe nerves, I skipped over to the wall and started touching it. It felt like a tree.

"Wow, it's like being outside inside."

I looked around the cabin. Who was this guy? He seemed young and old, scary and approachable, someone I wanted to know more about.

"Hey, what's your name, anyway? I'm Lilly, that's Joey, and that's his brother Barry."

The man inhaled and after a long pause he said, "Jic."

I looked up at the loft and noticed there were sun panels that were opened with screens, the warm breeze blowing through.

The road we had come on wasn't visible from this side of the house, only deep woods.

"What's in this direction?" I pointed away from where our car was.

Jic told us that after walking a few miles you would hit a small grocery store, gas pump, diner, and a bar. The rest was woods.

Joey was giving me mean looks; his face had gotten tight like I had never seen. I looked at him questioningly and shrugged my shoulders.

Barry asked about the sun panels, and he and Jic walked up the loft to look at them. I went over to Joey.

"What did I do?"

"You are so flirting with that guy it isn't funny."

I was astounded. Yes, Jic was a really interesting character and I wanted to know more, but I didn't think I was flirting.

"I'm sorry. I didn't think I was."

"Why don't you ask if you can live here with him? Barry and I will go on the road trip alone."

Now I was mad. "That is so stupid." Then I hugged him. "You are my boyfriend, no one else."

Barry and Jic walked back down from the loft.

"We should hit the road, guys. It's getting late and we have a couple of hours before we reach Chapel Hill," Joey said, lingering by the door.

Barry said to Jic, "We're going to visit a friend of mine who goes to the University. There's a party at his house tonight. Want to come? We can't drive you back cause we're going west from there."

Barry didn't see the fire in Joey's eyes but I did. What happened to that laid-back dude back in Newton? He seemed so secure and sure of himself. What was this?

Jic looked at us for a few minutes. He seemed to be thinking if it was worth his while.

Finally he nodded. "Sure. Chapel Hill is cool. Just let me close the windows."

He went up to the loft as Joey stormed out the door. Barry looked at me and rolled his eyes. "Moody bastard." He went out after him. Jic walked out with me, and if he sensed any tension his face sure didn't register it. He looked calm, strong, and extremely handsome.

Chapter Six

Sarah

I was sitting in the backseat with Jic, and Joey and Barry were up front. The radio was playing "Casey Jones" by The Grateful Dead. Jic had fallen fast asleep the minute we started driving. I think the music helped Joey with his jealousy fit since the Dead were his favorite band.

By evening we were in Chapel Hill, North Carolina, home to UNC amongst other places. The town looked a little like Harvard Square, with restaurants, lots of bookstores, cafes, and clothes stores.

We pulled into a driveway of this huge house on some dark street in back of the main road. I was glad Joey was navigating; I was very tired and had no idea where we were. And I was thinking a lot about Jessie.

"I'm starving. Can't we eat first?" It felt like a hundred hours since that bag of potato chips on the road south of nowhere.

"Buddy will have tons of food, he loves to eat," Barry said.

We were at the front door and Barry was knocking.

"Barry!"

"Buddy!"

Buddy was tall and about three hundred pounds. He had a huge smile on his pink flushed face and long brown hair that was in a ponytail.

"Friends! Come in to my humble abode!"

There was a party in full swing. Barry was right about the food: fried chicken, pizza, plates of hamburgers and hot dogs, and every snack you could imagine on this huge table in the front hall. There was a keg of beer surrounded by four guys who were having a chugging contest.

We got some plates and loaded up. Then we were led to Buddy's bedroom, a big room with strobe lights and a few people smoking reefer.

The clock on the wall of his bedroom was shaped like a football and had New England Patriots written on the face. It was two a.m. No wonder I was so tired.

After we stuffed our faces, Joey tried to pull me into a sleeping bag he found on the floor. I pushed him away. There were too many people around, no public sex for me. Since that time at Jamie's house, we had sex a few more times, and I made sure he wore a rubber. I liked it better each time. I think I was good at it too. Joey seemed pretty happy with the whole thing.

There was music playing in Buddy's room, and people were just lying around. Barry was talking about our trip. I didn't see Jic anywhere. I decided to look for him.

I walked downstairs into a big living room. There were two people sleeping on the couch and music playing something jazzy. The house had emptied out since we arrived.

I noticed that it was pretty clean, considering a bunch of college kids just had a party.

I found out the reason it was so clean when I walked into the kitchen. A pretty girl was furiously scrubbing the counter with this huge sponge. She was chewing gum a mile a minute. She was tall with long, dirty blond hair that was straight and messy, and was thin but not sickly thin. She looked at me intensely.

"Hi, who are you, I'm Sarah, I did way too much speed, and really need to come down if I'm ever going to sleep again, want to help, no, forget it, I like doing this myself, but you can help if you want, maybe you want some food, we have food in the fridge, I'm Buddy's girlfriend, actually, we broke up last week, but are still friends, see I think I'm a lesbian, so he doesn't mind, in fact, he said it's a turn-on, and lots of guys think that when they find out a girl is gay, which I just found out after falling in love with Liza, but she moved back to New York City, which I'm really bummed about, she wants me to move there too, but I still have another year, I'm a sociology major, yeah, I know, what kind of major is that, what are you, who are you, I've never seen you before, want some water, I do, I am so thirsty..."

She opened the refrigerator and took out a bottle of Coors Beer. She chugged about half of it and started coughing. I patted her on the back.

She took a deep breath. "Hi, I'm Sarah."

"Hi, I'm Lilly."

She had bright green eyes that were wide open and glassy.

"Lilly, see I'm working on this paper that I owe my professor, and I took all this speed thinking I would work through the night, you know, good start to the summer and all, even though I don't need to hand it in until September. Believe it or not, this project was going to be a study of what percentage of feminists turn into lesbians—well something like that—but I got sidetracked with personal stuff."

She chugged some of her beer and I just watched, enthralled by her monologue and the green sparkles of her eyes, getting brighter as she talked.

"My first topic was going to be about 'Schools without Walls,' you know, the sociological history and philosophy with evidence of how it affects future learning at the university level. I switched topics when I did a covert study of lesbianism and sat in on a coming-out group where I pretended I was confused and searching for answers, and I realized I was confused and searching for answers, this girl in the group, I mean woman, they like that word better, even though she's only nineteen like me, anyway, I fell in love with her for two weeks, and then she moved to New York. Right after we dyed our pubic hair. Want to see?"

Before I could respond, she pulled up her thin cotton dress. I was face-to-face with one little strip of pubic hair, bright purple. Sarah started laughing with her dimples shining on her cheeks as I looked away.

I thought I should say SOMETHING. "Um, how'd you end up with just a strip?"

Sarah dropped her dress and looked at me amazed.

"Don't tell me you've never heard of waxing?"

I shook my head.

"Where you been? You're sixteen or so?"

"Almost."

"You've never had the pleasure of having hot wax poured on your hairy body parts and then the hair ripped off with a piece of paper, like it's your skin?"

"Nope."

Sarah shook her head. "Wow. You don't know what you're missing." She giggled. "Well, let me see your legs."

Sarah grabbed one of my legs and lifted it up on the counter as I tried to balance myself by leaning against the stove. She ran her hand over my calf. I never shaved my legs because I hardly had any hair on them and what was there was light and mixed with my skin color so you couldn't see anything.

"Far-out! You are so lucky! No hair! Well I won't ask to see your pubes, since I just met you. Come on, let's go to my bedroom."

After the pubes and the feeling up of my leg, I didn't know what to expect, but I was so tired I just followed her. It was dark and she didn't turn on the light, just plopped down on her bed, which was huge, and took up the whole room except for a desk and a chair.

Her hands went under a pillow.

"Lilly, I'm sleeping now, you sleep too."

Her bare feet twitched a few times, and then her breathing steadied. I guessed she just wore herself out.

I was exhausted too. I took off my skirt, kept on my tee shirt and got between the sheets, which felt soft and cool. The pillows were deep and comfy. They smelled like oranges. I listened to the house sounds of people laughing upstairs in Buddy's room, music playing in the living room, and Sarah's breathing. I drifted off to a deep sleep.

I woke to someone kissing my neck. I looked to the right and saw Sarah, asleep, with her flowered dress. I looked to the left and there was Joey, kneeling on the side of the bed.

"Hey sexy girl, any room for me?"

There was light coming in the open curtains.

"What time is it?" I whispered.

"Nine. Who's the pretty girl?" He looked at me with his eyebrows raised.

I whispered, "It's not like that. I just met her."

He smiled again, bigger. "Is that so?"

I slapped his arm. "Not like that! Come on."

I got up and he followed me out of the room into the kitchen, making silly remarks about what he imagined.

The kitchen smelled like coffee and toast. Barry was sitting at the table with his maps, talking to Buddy about the next leg of our trip.

"Next stop is a campground outside of Baton Rouge, Louisiana. This will be the longest we go without stopping, about fourteen hours or so. We'll take turns sleeping and driving. We hit the road again right away, going to Austin, Texas. Play there for a bit, fun town I hear, next is New Mexico for some sightseeing, then on to Sunny California."

Buddy didn't look awake as he mumbled, "You gonna check out colleges?" He walked over to the sink to take a mouthful of water and gargled. "I have such a hangover. Beer and margaritas, I should know better."

He did look pretty bad, his face pale, hair stuck to his head, crusty.

Jic appeared out of nowhere. In direct contrast to Buddy, his hair looked just washed, wet and pulled back into a ponytail. It looked like he shaved around his beard and mustache, and he had on a clean white tee shirt, his muscles tight and peeking out of the short sleeves. He had a pack of Camels rolled in the left sleeve, and there was a tattoo coming out from his right shoulder. His eyes were shining that clear ocean blue as he surveyed the scene.

"Hey, Jic. Where you been?" I walked over to him and Joey followed me, putting his arm around me, which I found entirely unnecessary and completely annoying.

If Jic noticed anything, he didn't show it. "Hammock on the back porch. Great for sleeping." He picked up the coffee pot and looked at Buddy. "May I?"

Buddy mumbled, "No problem." Then he turned to Barry. "I'm going back to bed, man. Have a groovy trip." Buddy gave Barry a bear hug and stumbled out.

Joey sneered at Jic. "You sure know how to clear a room."

Jic poured his coffee and turned to Joey with his sideways smile. He nodded his head where Buddy just disappeared.

"Must have had a rough night."

Barry kept looking at his map. He seemed oblivious to Joey's hostility, whereas I felt like punching him. Instead, I made toast.

"Who wants some?" There was raspberry jam and I ate some from the jar.

"Oh, me, I love raspberry jam." We all looked up as Sarah bounced into the room.

"Hi, everyone." Sarah looked like she just slept for ten hours instead of the five that she did. Her long, blond hair was messy, and her face was fresh, her green eyes still glassy but not as unnaturally wide open.

She bounced over to me. "Hi, Lilly." She stuck her finger in the jam and hoisted herself onto the counter.

"Hi, Sarah."

Barry looked up and smiled. "Hi, Sarah."

Sarah kissed him on the cheek. "Hi, Barry."

Barry turned red. "OK, so, who's in? Jic, you want to keep going?"

Joey looked panicked and glared at Barry. "We have no room."

"Yeah we do. And we can use his woodsman skills." Then to Jic, "If you want to travel some more with us, that is."

If Jic noticed Joey's weirdness, he didn't show it. "Sure. I have friends out West."

I smiled with my head down.

Sarah jumped off the counter.

"You have space in the car? I want to come too! I am so done with this schoolwork. I need a vacation! I didn't know what was next, Buddy and I broke up, and we were going to the Outer Banks; now I have nothing to look forward to so I want to go with you! I'll be right back, just give me a minute to get my stuff, just some shampoo and stuff, that's all!"

Before anyone could say anything she ran upstairs.

Joey's mouth was open. "There's no way she can come."

Barry seemed to think the whole thing was funny. "We can always kick her out in Texas. Besides, she's cute."

With that, Barry grabbed his duffle bag that was leaning against the wall and threw it over his shoulder. "Let's go." He headed out to the car.

Jic took a last gulp of his coffee and followed Barry out of the house.

Joey just stood there.

"Come on, it will be fun," I said. I threw my arms around him and gave him a big kiss. He kissed me back and I got him to smile.

"It won't be fun but all right. At least I got you."

"You got me!" I said, happily, although I felt tightness around my neck like I was being strangled.

CHAPTER SEVEN

"You're
My Girlfriend"

Joey insisted on driving since that seat had the most room. Barry was shotgun reading his comic book, this time *Richie Rich*. In the back was me, Jic, and Sarah. Sarah had brought a huge suitcase, which was at our feet. All the rest of the stuff had to be squished in the small back, and we had to tie stuff like the sleeping bags and tents to the roof. Sarah was so happy to be with us, and her mood was contagious. Even Jic was wearing his sideways grin.

We were comparing hand sizes. I took out my journal for the first time and drew our hands.

"My first journal entry," I said.

"You should date it!" Sarah said. She took my pen and wrote "*June 29, 1978*."

Jic reached for the pen and turned to the first page that was empty. He drew a picture of a snake that looked exactly like the one that almost killed me. Beside it he wrote *"Jic's place, North Carolina: June 28, 1978."*

The Allman Brothers were on the radio playing, "In Memory of Elizabeth Reed." The song was beautiful and Duane Allman made the guitar sound like it was weeping.

Right before we fell asleep, I told everyone I was going to be the fire maker. They were cool with that. I loved everything about making fires—the striking of the match, the second before it lights, the sizzle, and especially the smoky, woodsy smell.

The ride to Baton Rouge took thirteen hours and we got there after midnight. Joey managed to get the bug up to seventy mph as did Jic and Barry. Sarah didn't want to drive and I took a short shift going sixty-five. We had pee and food breaks, everyone getting their favorites: me cheese puffs and Tab, Joey Oreos and milk, Barry Captain Crunch and milk, Sarah anything salty like potato chips or pretzels and Tab, and Jic a burger or tuna sandwich with Coke.

When it was my turn to drive, Sarah sat up front with me and talked my ear off. She must have popped more speed.

"I miss Buddy. He was a good friend. We went out for about a year. I met him the first day of classes; he was in my women's history class. Said he was there to meet girls since mostly girls signed up! Wrong class to meet girls, though; most of them were feminists or becoming feminists and angry with men. Buddy and I would go out for cheesy fries after class and count how many anti-men comments were said that day. Or how many women were growing mustaches! Anyway, there was this girl, Liza, and she was really funny and would laugh at all the angry girls and tell them that in order to be equal to men they shouldn't hate them; they had to have compassion and love. She was pretty with really short, white-blond hair and she wore hip-huggers with halters, showing flat stomach and big boobs, which drove the feminists crazy. She was wild. She was the one who dyed my pubes purple. She had a tattoo of a unicorn on her back."

I took a swig of my Tab that was warm but still bubbly. "Did you…were you…just friends with her or did you… you know…"

Sarah laughed and threw her head back. "Did we have sex? Yeah, right before she left for New York. Only one time and it was really hot! She knew exactly where to touch, where to put her tongue, what to do with her fin…."

"It's OK! No details!"

"I fell so in love with her. And then she left."

"Don't you keep in touch?"

Sarah shrugged. "She's in a band in the city and has a girlfriend she's living with in the East Village. Maybe I'll visit some day."

I nodded for lack of anything to say. I'd never been in love like that. I thought I was in love with Joey in Newton and now, on the road somewhere between Chapel Hill and Baton Rouge, I didn't know how I felt.

Sarah leaned against the window and fell asleep. I was alone with my thoughts and of course they went to Jessie. Thinking of her and my Mom moving their stuff to the beach house. Wondering if she was still hiding her food in her napkin at dinner. Wondering about everything. I would call her when we got to Austin. I would tell her about my adventures and make sure she was OK.

Barry drove the last leg and then we pulled into the KOA campground outside of Baton Rouge, Louisiana. We could have been Anywhere, USA. It was dark out and sort of misty.

After finding a camping spot by a fire pit, we unpacked the car. I put myself in charge of lighting the fire. Jic, Barry, and Joey set up the tents and Sarah helped me find dry wood. We had a paper that we put in the fire and soon it was blazing.

We heated up beans in the can for a meal. For some reason, that was all the food we had.

"I thought you packed food." Barry looked at Joey in disgust.

"I thought *you* packed food."

"So where did these stinkin' beans come from?"

"Hey, don't insult my beans. It's a family recipe." Jic smiled as he held up the can of Heinz beans.

I pointed to the can. "Really? Your last name is Heinz?"

Jic just smiled and Joey hit the back of my head.

"Ow! What's your problem?"

"You are so gullible."

"Well don't hit me!"

I didn't see the point in hitting me. He could have been a Heinz. No one knew much about him.

Joey started complaining about being exhausted and having to sleep three to a tent since we only had two tents; he wanted to be alone with me. Sarah wished she had more speed for the next day. Even Barry started complaining; he was upset about the lack of real food.

The bad moods seemed contagious. I felt sad, missing my sister and worrying about how she was doing. Only Jic seemed unaffected, sitting on a log by the fire, cleaning his fingernails with his buck knife.

I went off by myself and lit a candle beside a tree. I took out my pen and journal and wrote:

Usually in the summer I am boogie boarding at Nantasket Beach with my sister and brother. The waves are gentle with no undertow. Heat lightening rises up from nowhere. A storm would be rising up today. Maybe my sister is in the middle of a storm that she can't get out of. She's caught and I have to save her. But I'm not there. So she's getting deeper into the bad weather and even a tornado. And here I am camping, going the other direction of the storm. How could that be right? I feel the wind here, on my back. Whipping. Maybe it's trying to whisper, or yell to me. Sucker! We got her!

There was snapping in the bushes. Was Joey looking for me again? I felt irritated.

"Whatcha doing?"

I turned around and it was Jic. I smiled without thinking and said, "Just some writing. What's everyone doing?"

"Sleeping. Joey's in one tent, Barry and Sarah in the other. I'm sleeping out here."

I got up and we walked to the fire together. We sat on a log. Jic rolled a cigarette from a bag of Bugler tobacco. He offered me some water from the canteen. It tasted good and a little tinny.

I guess my mouth was drawn down from writing about my sister. Jic noticed.

"You sad?" His eyes were warm and reflected the fire.

I nodded. "Yeah. Just family stuff."

He lit his cigarette and we looked into the fire.

I asked him, "You got family?"

"Some."

"Can you tell me about them? I don't want to think about me anymore."

He laughed. "Not that much to tell."

"Are you from North Carolina, is that where your parents are?"

He didn't answer for a while, just smoked, as the fire crackled.

"No."

"No what, I forget what I asked."

We both laughed.

"No they don't live in North Carolina."

A wind came up, sparks flew up, and I drew my flannel shirt closer.

"Now you're supposed to tell me where they live."

"Am I?"

There was a huge crack and one yellow spark flew up. It looked amazing in contrast with the black sky.

Jic flicked his cigarette in the fire and got to his feet. He looked at the fire once, turned to me and lifted a piece of my hair, giving it a gentle pull.

"Good night, Lilly."

I watched him as he grabbed a sleeping bag and went into the woods.

I stayed there alone before I thought of snakes and bears. I hightailed it into the tent. Joey was alone and I was grateful he was asleep. I was so tired I climbed into the sleeping bag that was graciously left for me and fell asleep in about three seconds flat.

I was in the middle of a dream where I was swimming in the ocean when I was interrupted by a yell from the other tent. Sarah.

"There's a bat in here!"

Joey groaned next to me. "What?"

"It's Sarah. Go back to sleep."

I struggled out of my sleeping bag and out of the tent. I was surprised to see it was light out, morning already. Sarah was shrieking and Barry was telling her to shut up.

Sarah was outside her tent jumping up and down yelling. It was freezing.

She looked up. "Lilly, help! Get these bugs off me!" She was in her underwear and a tee shirt, shaking her long hair and picking at it.

"Stop. Calm down and let me see."

She stood still and I looked through her hair. I pulled out a few leaves.

"No bugs. Just leaves." I showed her.

"There were bugs in my hair. And a bat."

"It's freezing out here!"

She ran into her tent, pulled out her sleeping bag, and put it next to one of the large trees we camped next to. She climbed in and opened it up for me. I was freezing too, so I climbed in and she zipped it up. It was so warm right away.

"I think I'm crashing from all the speed I did yesterday," she whispered to me, as the breezes flew by our faces, tickling our noses, lighting the sky another orange glow.

"Probably should have brought some with me. You do anything?"

Her face was so close I couldn't see her so I backed up as much as I could.

"Nah. It doesn't attract me."

She laughed. "Well, boys attract you. At least, you attract them."

We heard a crunching of dirt from the tents.

I peeked out and saw Barry, his pants unzipped, scratching his beard.

"What are you lezzies laughing about?" He went behind us and started to pee. We both sat up in the sleeping bag.

Sarah yelled, "Gross! Go into the woods, you pig!"

"It's my car," Barry said.

Sarah and I looked at each other and laughed. I got out of the bag.

"That makes no sense, Barry."

He zipped up his pants and straightened his glasses.

"Yeah, well, I need some coffee. Real coffee, not this instant shit. There must be a diner near here. Let's get some real breakfast."

He looked into the sky and yelled, "Breakfast everyone! Wake up!"

Jic walked out of the woods. He looked cleanly shaven and fresh. He nodded to us and walked toward the fire that was now out.

"Is there a hotel in the woods or something? How do you always look so good?" I asked him.

Jic smiled the half-smile and Barry glared at me. I felt myself get hot. I guess I shouldn't have said that. After all, I was supposed to be Joey's girl.

With that thought I ran into the tent and jumped on Joey in his bag. "Wake up, we're going for breakfast!"

He grabbed me and we rolled around the tent until Barry kicked it and yelled at us to get going.

Within twenty minutes the car was packed, camping stuff tied to the roof, Barry at the wheel. With the anticipation of eggs, bacon, coffee, and pancakes, everyone was happier.

I had on my short jean shorts with my red Bogart's bar tee shirt underneath the warm flannel shirt. I looked at my thigh and noticed a long scratch from the knee up. Jic and Sarah noticed it too. Jic was sitting in the middle of us. "How far up does that go?" he asked with his smile.

I shrugged and traced my finger along it as they watched. The scratch turned in and went up where they didn't need to look.

"Oops," I said as I pulled my shorts back.

Jic's blue eyes flashed happy as he said, "Nice scratch."

Sarah said, "See, that's why you have to wax. Although, I didn't see any pubes."

Jic said, "Pubic hair is sexy. Don't wax it off."

I was astonished. How did this country boy know about waxing?

"Sexy?" Sarah looked at him amazed.

"The right amount is sexy."

Sarah considered. "OK, well, I'll leave some on you then, Lilly. Just a strip."

I shook my head. "Did you pack a waxing kit in your suitcase or something?"

Barry pulled into a roadside dinner and yelled, "Get ready for some real food!"

The parking lot was full of pickups, vans, trucks, regular cars, and a few motorcycles.

We all piled out. Joey came right over to me and put his arm around me.

"What were you talking about in the backseat?"

I pulled away from his arm.

"Just girl stuff."

We walked into the diner as Joey mumbled, "Jic's not a girl."

I chose to ignore him, following Sarah. The diner was crowded. Families, truckers, bikers, everyone seemed to be in this restaurant. There was a long counter with folks sitting on stools.

Sarah pointed to an empty booth. "Let's sit here." As we walked over, people stared at us. I guessed there were lots of locals. The food smelled great.

Joey grabbed my arm. "Sit next to me."

"OK."

Sarah gave me a strange look and giggled. This possessive stuff was starting to be annoying. When I sat next to him, he put his hand on my thigh and felt the scratch.

"Where'd you get that?"

I shrugged.

"Is that what you guys were talking about? Your scratch?"

The waitress came, a soft-talking woman with big, blond hair and a flowered apron, and brought menus.

We ordered everything on the menu that was breakfast-like. Soon there was coffee and juice, eggs, pancakes, bacon, and sausage piled in front of us.

We ate ferociously. Barry looked so happy eating. In between bites he talked about our next stop, Austin, Texas.

"We should get there around ten tonight, if we don't stop much. Austin is a wicked good place to hear music, and there's lots of Mexican food."

Sarah was in a happy mood and seemed to be over her bug episode. She was telling Barry to piss DEEP in the woods and not on her head.

I piped in. "Yeah, no one wants to see your wiener."

Sarah looked at me. "Weiner? What are you, eight years old?"

Jic did his stare/half-smile thing at Sarah and said, "Barry, watch out for this girl. She has no pubic hair."

The three of us cracked up. Barry stuffed a sausage in his mouth and let half of it hang out.

"Disgusting!" Sarah threw a piece of toast at him and it landed on Jic's plate.

Jic picked it up and ate it. "Thanks, I was looking for more toast."

I smiled at Jic and he winked.

Joey banged down his coffee cup and glared at me. "Is that what you were talking about in the car? Pubic hair?" He glared at Jic, who took a sip of coffee and looked calmly at Joey.

Joey's voice got louder. "Why are you doing this?"

"I'm not doing anything," I said quietly. What was I doing?

Jic tilted his head to the side and said to Joey, "What exactly is your problem?"

Joey stood up, spilling my coffee as he pointed at Jic and yelled, "My problem is that YOU want to ball my girlfriend!"

Now Jic stood up, facing Joey. "Oh, is that right?"

The waitress came running over, her yellow hair bobbing and her lips quivering. A man in the next booth was sitting with a woman, and he was shaking his head at us. Two truck-driver-looking guys at the counter were laughing and watching.

"Young man, you can't use that language in here. This is a family establishment. Please calm down, or you will have to leave."

Barry tugged at Joey's arm. "Yeah, young man. This is a family establishment. You're scaring the kids."

Joey pushed him away and was out the door in a flash. Jic sat back down, and Sarah flicked a potato at me. "Go after him."

When I got outside I couldn't locate Joey. Not in the parking lot, not around back. I went back inside, thinking maybe he ran back in, but no Joey.

Then I saw him leaning against the hood of our car. I felt bad and also mad for something I didn't really understand.

I walked over and put my hand in his hair, something I knew he liked. He pulled away.

"What did I do?"

"You don't know?"

I shrugged. "I was just being friendly."

He finally looked into my eyes. His eyes were wet.

"Lilly, I invited you on this trip. You came on this trip with ME. And you're not acting like my girlfriend. You act like no one's girlfriend."

The outside light changed. Extremely bright turned into deep darkness as the sun moved behind a black cloud. Then it started to pour. We ran for cover by the front door.

I looked at him and tried to see the cute boy I fell in love with only a month ago.

"Sorry. I didn't realize I was doing anything."

"Well realize it. You're my girlfriend, so act like it."

My mouth must have dropped open because Barry came out of the door and said, "Lilly, you're catching flies." Then he stuck his hand out. "Five bucks each for the food."

We paid him and I watched as Joey walked to the car and sat in the backseat, not even looking at me. I stood outside and watched the storm.

Sarah came out first and put her arm around me. "Everything all right?"

I shrugged. "Not really, he's being a jerk. Am I flirting with Jic?"

She laughed. "Is that what he said?"

I nodded.

She shook her head. "It doesn't seem that way to me. But what do I know." She grabbed my hand. "Just hang with me; I'll keep you out of trouble."

I pushed her with my hip. "Yeah, right. Come on, let's run to the car."

It was still pouring pretty hard. Barry and Jic were walking behind us. At the car Barry announced that he was going to sleep in the back since Sarah kicked him all night and screamed him awake in the morning. Sarah stuck her tongue out and piled in next to him, saying she didn't sleep either because of the bat and was going to use him as a pillow. So that left Jic and me in the front, Jic taking the wheel.

All those pancakes settled in my stomach. I felt sleepy and also wanted to talk with Jic. I wondered if he felt weird toward me because of the scene in the diner. I tried to make light conversation and, as usual, he didn't talk much. So everything was status quo. Exhaustion took over and I fell asleep, my head against the window. When I woke up, it was dark out. Jic was still driving and chewing something, his LA Lakers hat pulled down low.

"What time is it?"

He glanced at me and half-smiled.

"Eight o'clock, mountain time."

"Wow. I slept too long."

I turned my body sideways so I could see him better. He was eating Milk Duds. I found the box next to him and took one.

"These and 3 Musketeers bars are my favorite," I said.

"Frozen Milky Ways."

"Absolutely."

"Aren't you tired of driving? Where are we?"

"Closing in on Texas, I expect."

I took another Milk Dud and looked at the long, flat road ahead. "Barry says we'll stop for a couple days in Austin and then a week or so in New Mexico."

Jic took a cigarette from his pack of Camels with his left hand as he kept his right hand on the wheel. When it was in his mouth, he punched in the car lighter.

"You guys are just driving through, not sightseeing. There's a lot of great stuff to see. What's the point of your trip?"

I thought about that. I didn't really know what the point was.

"Well, my point was to escape summer with my family. Except I feel worried about my sister."

"Call her."

"Yeah, I will when we get to Austin."

One of the things I liked about Jic was he didn't ask about stuff; he waited for you to offer the information. And I didn't feel like getting into the thing with my sister, so I didn't.

"You went across country before?"

Jic's lighter popped out. He nodded as he lit his cigarette. "Yeah, back and forth from the East. A few summers ago. There are some really amazing places to see."

"Like?"

"Well, the Grand Canyon, for one. Carlsbad Caverns, since you'll be in New Mexico. The desert. Lots of stuff."

I thought about that. Now I wanted to go sightseeing.

"Maybe you can take us to the caves in New Mexico."

He shrugged. "Maybe."

I had been wondering about something since I met Jic, and I thought now would be a good time to ask.

"Don't you have any people?"

"People?"

"Yeah, like, parents, friends, siblings. I never hear you talk about anyone."

There was a long silence.

"Yeah, I have people. My parents are in New York; I have friends there and in LA. North Carolina is a getaway place."

I tried to be cool about my next question, but it came out too loudly. "Where does your girlfriend live, East or West?"

There was movement in the backseat. I glanced back; it was Sarah, readjusting, going back to sleep.

He smiled that sly smile and glanced at me.

"What? I was just wondering."

"One on each coast. At least."

I punched his arm lightly. "Very funny."

I turned my body and looked ahead. The road was straight and dark with hardly any lights on it. We were the only car in sight.

I leaned in toward him and he took a handful of my hair, twirling it around his fingers.

"Your turn to drive."

"Sure. You've been driving for so long."

He pulled over. We both got out and stood by the side of the road while everyone slept. The sky was dark with thousands of stars. The air smelled like fresh stream water. We stood together staring up.

"Over that ridge is Texas." He nodded to the left.

"Wow. It's so close."

Jic nodded.

A shooting star flew across the sky, leaving a trail of floating sparkles.

I jumped and pointed, excited. "Did you see that?"

"Yeah."

"Supposed to wish upon it!"

He looked at me and said, "OK. Wish upon it then. Out loud."

It was a challenge. I turned to him, closed and opened my eyes, and said, "I wish that when I get back home, my sister is all better."

Wishing that made me sad and, without wanting to, I started to cry.

Jic stepped close to me and wiped my tears with his finger. He put my hair behind my ear and smiled at me.

"I hope she's better too."

I looked at him and every atom in my body wanted to be in his arms. I glanced at the car and reminded myself that I was Joey's girlfriend on this trip.

"Your wish, Jic?" It came out soft and small and he stood closer to me but with his hands in his pockets.

After a frustratingly long pause, he said, "The thing in New York to resolve."

He looked toward Texas.

"Explain?"

He took a cigarette from the back of his ear, a wooden match from his pocket that he lit on the heel of his boot, and lit up.

"Time to drive."

We got in and Jic found a radio station playing country music, some sad song. I opened a can of Tab and started to drive. Jic pulled his cap down and smoked. I thought about all that I knew about him, which was next to nothing. Found him in a cabin in North Carolina, shot snakes, put them on his walls, had family in New York and friends in LA?

I looked at him sideways. His head was against the window and he was sleeping. Everyone was sleeping. Time to drive and think about where I was going. Texas! And then, New Mexico! With red dirt and roadside stands, like my dream. My body was getting tan, my hair was streaked with blond from the sun, and I felt there was some awesome adventure waiting for us, just down the highway.

CHAPTER EIGHT

Armadillo World Headquarters

Everyone woke up right outside of Austin. We decided to spring for a motel room so we could take real showers and sleep in real beds. Barry and Jic got the room, and the rest of us snuck in. We took showers and then went out to explore the town. It was some time after midnight, and there were lots of people out.

Barry had heard about a place called Armadillo World Headquarters, a famous music dance place. It was in an old armory that someone had turned into a music hall. We walked through town and found it on a back street. We got in no problem, no IDs checked, and the place was buzzing with people. There were cowboys, hippies, and regular businessmen with their ties and jackets, and everyone was dancing!

We found a place to stand by the long bar. Barry stood by a bowl of peanuts and ordered us Lone Star beers. Joey was talking with a hippie with long, blond hair and a tie-dyed headband. The band was really loud and good. Their name was New Riders of the Purple Sage, but I had never heard of them.

"Let's dance!" Sarah grabbed my hand and we went out to the dance floor. It was really crowded. It felt great to move after all those hours in the car. Jic leaned against the bar and took in the scene.

After a long while dancing, we took a break. I don't usually like beer, but Lone Star tasted cold and great. We ordered big bowls of chili that came with melted cheese and chips. Spicy and delicious!

"Where did Joey go?" I had to shout over the music to Barry.

"He said something about mushrooms and went off with some guy. He better not disappear." Barry dipped a taco chip into his chili.

We stayed at Armadillo World Headquarters until early morning, dancing, eating, drinking, and having fun. Sarah and I danced together. Guys would dance and talk with us but we always went back to Jic and Barry at the bar, our safe haven.

Joey came back after a couple of hours, really high on mushrooms, weed, and wine. He grabbed me on the dance floor and started twirling me around. It was fun until he ran outside to puke.

Joey leaned against the side of the building. The air was warm and humid. Stars were dull. No one was around except us.

"Wow, mushrooms and wine always do that to me."

He looked wasted and gross so I kept my distance.

"My parents are in Europe now. They are so out-of-touch. Lilly, wait until you meet them. Out to lunch. They need to wake up."

I wanted to say that maybe he was sleeping, being stoned all the time, but that wasn't a girlfriend thing to say. I was trying to act like a better girlfriend since the episode, but he had barf on his cheek and eyes the size of teacups.

"Yeah, well, wipe your face, Joey, and let's go back in."

He sat on the ground. "I'll be in."

Back inside I told Barry about Joey.

"What an asshole." He said a few more choice words and went out to see him.

A few minutes later Barry came back in and looked disgusted. "I'm going back to the motel. Joey is such a pain in the ass! He does too many of whatever he puts in his mouth! I should just leave him in his own vomit." Barry was screaming over the music.

Sarah and I leaned against the bar. I knew I should help, but I didn't want to leave, or be around Joey.

Sarah, who hadn't stopped smiling since we hit Austin, kissed Barry on the cheek. "I'll help you."

He shook his head. "Maybe I'll come back. It's not that far away. Or maybe I'll leave him in the middle of the street to get run over."

He walked out.

"Sarah, should we go?" I had to scream over the music.

"Soon. Two more dances."

She grabbed me for another dance. New Riders played great music. I closed my eyes and pretended I was alone with just the music.

They started playing a slow bluesy song. Sarah put her arms around me and her cheek up to mine.

I giggled and looked in her eyes. "What are you doing?"

She smiled. "Just snuggling. Nothing." She moved in again.

A cowboy came up to us. "Can we cut in? I'm sure you ladies would rather dance with us."

I looked up and there was a really tall guy, standing with a couple of other cowboys, clad in hats and jean jackets with bandanas around their thick necks. They looked like a Wild West movie. I didn't like how they were leering at us, looking us up and down and smiling like they wanted to eat us up.

"It's OK. We were just going. Thanks anyway!" I grabbed Sarah and ran to the bar to find Jic. They followed us to where Jic was talking with a pretty bartender.

Jic looked up.

I motioned to the guys coming up behind us. "We want to go!"

Jic assessed the scene and nodded. He said good-bye to the bartender who wrote something on a piece of paper and gave it to him.

On our way out I whispered, "We didn't do anything. We were just dancing."

Outside the air was cooler and it was beginning to get light. It must have been morning already.

The three men had followed us outside. Jic stopped and turned to face them. They looked at him, looked at us, laughed, and walked to the parking lot. I let out my breath that had been stuck in my throat.

"Harmless dudes." Jic put his arm around both of us and we walked through Austin back to our motel room.

The city was clean and awake. People were walking with cups of coffee or driving in their pickups or cars. I wondered what day it was.

We reached the motel room. I was so tired; I climbed into one of the cots. Joey was on a chair half-asleep with his guitar in his hand, and Barry was asleep in one of the beds. Sarah climbed into a cot next to me and Jic took the bed next to Barry.

"Gonna call that bartender?" I said to Jic.

He threw a pillow at me. "Shut up and go to sleep or I'll tell those cowboys to come get you."

I fell asleep, deep and smiling.

Chapter Nine

New Mexico

"I should put you on a plane back to Boston!"

I woke up to Barry's loud voice. He was lying in bed looking up at Joey who was just out of the shower with a towel around his waist.

Joey sat on the edge of the bed. "Bro, I'm sorry! It was the wine! I won't drink wine anymore!"

Barry stood up and headed to the bathroom. "Yeah, what about the mushrooms and the weed? You make me sick."

He slammed the door and we heard the shower go on.

Joey came over to my cot. He smelled clean, which I was thankful for.

"Hey, Lilly, you're not mad at me, are you?" He leaned his wet head against my chest.

I had no idea what to say. So I kissed him and then pushed him off me. It was about one hundred degrees in the room.

"What time is it?" I looked at the window but the curtains looked dark.

"Ten or so. We slept long."

"AM or PM?"

I walked to the window and looked out. It was dark. Some cars were pulling out of the parking lot. The motel VACANCY sign flashed orange.

"It's night?" Sarah was sitting up in her bed. She looked over at Joey who was pulling on his jeans, his bare butt flashing.

"Thanks for the moonlight. Are you feeling better?"

Joey grinned as he pulled on his pants. "Totally. Never really felt bad."

Sarah pulled her hair back. "Well, you ruined Barry's night. He had to bring you back here after you puked all over the parking lot. He had to babysit you. Not very cool."

Joey's grin disappeared. "I didn't ask him to."

Sarah looked at me and I shrugged. It was confusing to know what to do or say.

"Shoot! I have to call my house! What time is it in Boston?"

Sarah looked at the clock radio. "Like eleven."

I picked up the phone and called the beach house collect. No one answered. I called Newton. Still no answer. It was late; maybe they were sleeping. I would try again at our next stop.

Everyone showered and we packed up the car. We walked over to the Austin Lights diner that was next to the motel.

I didn't know whether to order breakfast or dinner. So I ordered a grilled cheese. Barry and Jic ordered steaks, Sarah had eggs, and Joey had a burger.

"So we'll drive straight to the KOA campground outside of Carlsbad, New Mexico. A friend of mine stayed there last summer and said it was great, with a huge lake and lots of cool people. We'll stay for July Fourth and then hit the road again. It will take about ten hours, so we'll get there in the morning."

"We should stay in Austin a few more days," Joey said.

Barry took a gulp of his coffee. "Be my guest. We'll pick you up in about three weeks, on our way home."

Jic lit a cigarette. "Just be careful; don't get lost in the city."

We all took up the tease.

"I'll miss you!" I hugged him and kissed him big on the lips.

"I won't." Sarah flung her hair.

Joey looked confused. "I meant with everyone, not alone. But I don't want to miss New Mexico, either."

We got up to pay the check. Joey trailed behind, looking worried.

As he followed us to the car, I took his hand. "Joey, we were kidding! We wouldn't leave you."

His lip was jutted out and he walked slowly. When we got to the car, Barry hit him playfully on the head.

"Get in. Just behave!"

When we decided who would drive (Barry first shift, Jic second) I whispered to Sarah, "Was that mean?"

"He deserved it."

The hours flew by as fast as the scenery. We stopped twice for pee breaks and snacks. People slept more. I fell asleep midway, after looking out the window trying to find shooting stars.

When we crossed the border into New Mexico, Sarah screamed, "We're here!"

Jic was driving, his elbow out the window. It was early morning and there was a warm breeze blowing. We opened all the windows. Barry started shouting directions to the campground. Joey was in a better mood from sleep, and Sarah was antsy to swim, run, anything but sitting.

An hour later we pulled into the campground. We parked at the office. A small wooden sign on the door said, "Welcome to Lu-Anne's."

"I thought it was a KOA." Barry checked his directions.

Sarah said, "Maybe they got bought out. Let's just go!"

Walking to the office, I saw kids running around and some hippies at their campsites. We opened the door and were greeted by a large woman wearing a tie-dyed dress, her hair in pigtails down to her belly and a leather band around her forehead. She had a feather necklace, and when she smiled, most of her back teeth were missing. She told us her name was Lu-Anne, and the smell of patchouli oil filled the air around her when she moved. She gave us a box of Fruit Loops with a map of the place, pointing to the area our cabin would be.

"No keys, so I would lock any valuables in your car. Most everyone is nice, but we have had a few thieves over the years, heh heh heh." Her laugh came out the side of her mouth and her head bobbed with it. Barry was already out the door with the cereal, Joey following. Jic, Sarah, and I wanted to talk with her some more.

"If you're around for July Fourth we have a big party by the lake, which is that way," she looked out her window and motioned to the right. "The map tells all. I drew it. Pretty good, I think. Heh, heh, heh."

Sarah snickered and I nudged her. Jic tipped his Lakers hat and said, "Thank you very much for all your help." He turned, glancing at us to follow, and we did.

I ran after him. "She was great. She's my big fat Momma, the one I wrote about."

He looked at me strangely, and I realized he didn't know what I was talking about.

"Oh. I wrote about her in my diary. Before I came here! I bet she bakes muffins one day!" I skipped along, I was so happy. The campground felt like a good place, and I was relieved to be somewhere that we would stay for a while.

We had decided to treat ourselves to a cabin instead of using tents. It was a two-bedroom log cabin with two bunk beds in each room, a bathroom with a shower, and a big room with a wooden table to eat at, two long benches for seating, kitchen area, and fireplace. I loved it. It felt homey.

We unpacked the car and organized our rooms. Joey and me in one room and Barry, Jic, and Sarah in the other.

We pushed beds together.

Joey was so happy that we had our own room. He pushed me on the bed and jumped playfully on top of me. He started singing, "I think we're alone now. There doesn't seem to be anyone around."

I laughed as he tickled me.

Sarah stuck her head in. "Get a room, you two. Oh, that's right, you have one."

Joey kissed me a long time and it felt nice. But I was too excited to explore the campground, so I jumped up and pulled his arm. "Let's explore and do this later!"

He put his arm around me and we went outside.

There was a picnic table twenty feet from the front door, with a charcoal grill and a pit for a campfire. There was a path that we thought led down to the lake.

"Let's go see the lake!" I took Joey's hand.

Barry was coming from the car with Joey's guitar and Sarah's pillow. He handed the guitar to Joey and threw the pillow at Sarah, who was coming out of the cabin.

"My pillow! Thanks! Hey, let's have a meeting at the picnic table!"

Barry snarled. "What the hell is a meeting?"

Sarah flung her hair back. It was so dirty it looked brown. "We talk, jerk off."

She got everyone to sit around the table. Jic opened his buck knife and picked at the dirt under his fingernails. Joey was rolling a joint, all excited about finding his stash in a sleeping bag. Barry had the box of Fruit Loops and was stuffing them in his face. I watched Sarah.

She twirled her hair and sat cross-legged. "I just thought it would be good to talk about our trip and discuss how long everyone wants to stay here and what we will do here, like, maybe seeing some sights, and where our next stop will be. I mean, I'm along for the ride and it's really great of you guys to take me, but I wanted to know how far you are going, are you staying here for a while, and, well, do you think we could find some speed around here?"

Barry laughed. "Oh, so it's a speed thing. I should have known. You jonesing dyke girl?"

"Don't call me dyke girl! I don't know which way I'm going. Plus I'm not butch. Am I?" She turned to me. "Lilly, do I look manly? I don't, do I? Look at my boobs," she pulled up her shirt. "They stand straight up. And my face is feminine. And look at my…"

I stopped her from pulling down her shorts and showing anything else. "Sarah! You know you aren't butchy! Look how much Barry is drooling. He just wants you to strip, so stop!"

Barry laughed, happy at the show. He even put down his box of Fruit Loops. "You're gorgeous. I'm just wondering why you would go for girls. What a waste."

Sarah stuck her tongue out. "And I'm not a speed freak. It's just that, I like it. So, will you help me find some or what?"

A kid about four years old ran by, laughing, looking back. He had long hair, no shirt, bare feet, and shorts. A few seconds later a tall man ran after him, also with long hair with a ponytail, dressed just like the kid. He put his fingers in a peace sign when he saw us and smiled.

I waved. "Friendly neighbors."

Sarah looked down the path where they ran. "Maybe that guy knows where we can get some stuff. At least point us in the right direction. This looks like a party campground."

Barry got up, holding the box of cereal close to his body. "Well, I'm taking a shower. You can go chase rodeo men for all I care, or, rodeo women, whatever turns you on. Hey, good meeting, Sarah."

He walked into the cabin.

I poked Joey in the side. "Your brother can be a real jerk."

Joey shrugged and stood up. "Sarah, I'll go with you. I want to see about some acid. This looks like the perfect place to trip." He looked happy like back at home and relaxed. He kissed me on the cheek and grabbed his guitar. They walked in the direction of the man and his kid, which left Jic and me at the table.

Jic folded up his knife, stretched out his arms, and stood. "I'm going to look around."

Which left me sitting at the table all alone. I looked up and there was huge sky, unlike any other I had ever seen. In the distance were mountains. Close by were rock cliffs. Around me were trees and voices, echoes, laughing. Smoke and burger smell lingered in the air.

Where was my sister now? Was she eating okay? Was she at the beach, was she having fun with our friends, did she have a new boyfriend? How was my father's business trip? What was my mother doing? How were the sandcastles I used to make, the dribble castles? Were all the kids I knew bodysurfing, making bonfires, getting ready for the Fourth of July fireworks? My mom was always happier at the beach. She was probably making a barbecue and playing Scrabble with my sister, having her friends over, making jokes, smiling. Without my father there, my mother always seemed happier, freer. Why wasn't I there? Why did I come on this road trip, to miss the beach, to miss the summer in the waves? The ocean was my favorite place on earth. And here I was at a campground somewhere in New Mexico, no ocean in sight, with a jealous boyfriend, a speed-freak girl, a wisecracker guy, and a mysterious hunk of a boy who

I would follow to the ends of the earth. What was going on?

Barry came out of the cabin, his hair wet, with clean clothes on. He had a bottle of Boone's Farm Apple wine in his hand that he must have been stashing in the car.

"Come on, moody, let's go find my brother."

The way he said it was nice, like he was noticing how I felt, and it made me happy, like someone was watching. I followed him down the path toward the music and voices. We went through some trees and then to the next campground. Milling around a campfire was a bunch of people. The guy with the ponytail we saw before, another guitar player with a mustache, the little boy playing in a sandpile with a girl in a cotton dress, a woman with a cowboy hat in a bikini top with a long skirt who was making peanut butter sandwiches, and then Joey and Sarah, smoking a joint and sitting on a bench.

Joey moved over on the bench and put his arm around me.

"Lilly, Barry, meet our new friends. This is Charlie and his wife Sandy," the ponytail guy and the bikini woman smiled and said hi; the guy playing the guitar was Liquid. The boy was River and the girl was Blossom.

Barry passed around the bottle of Boone's Farm, and Joey rolled another joint.

Charlie was holding a piece of paper. I noticed there were small inkblots of the trucker guy by the artist R. Crumb.

There were about fifty of these little trucker guys. Charlie started to cut them into squares. Sandy came over to the table. She was tall and slim, like Charlie, with light brown, wavy hair and a pretty smile. There was a smell of peanut butter about her.

"Are those your kids?" I nodded to the sandpile.

"The boy. The girl is from the next campground. Her parents went to town for supplies. Real nice people, from New Hampshire." She licked peanut butter off her thumb. "Where are you all from?"

"Boston area, Newton. How about you?"

"In between homes. We are deciding whether to move to California, where Charlie is from, or back east to Vermont where I grew up. So for now, this is home." She smiled and turned to Charlie.

"Hey, baby, make sure you don't leave that stuff out. We don't want the kids to get it."

Charlie laughed and nodded. "That would be some acid trip."

She turned serious. "Not funny."

He kissed her. "I'll be careful, babe. Most of it will be gone soon. It's my Fourth of July present to anyone who wants it. And I know this guy here," he pointed to Joey, "wants it."

"Damn straight!" Joey did a high five with him and squeezed my arm. "Told you I would find some."

Sandy walked over to the children with sandwiches and spread out a blanket near the sandbox. I watched the kids dance over. They were so innocent-looking, it felt weird to have acid, reefer, and wine so near to them. They didn't seem to notice.

Through the trees there was a path that went to the lake. It was getting warmer and I was sweaty.

I leaned over to Joey. "I'm going to check out the lake. Want to come?"

He had a reefer in one hand and some of the blotter acid in another. "Nah, I'll just hang here."

"Are you gonna trip now?"

"Probably wait until tomorrow. Fourth of July! Everyone will be tripping. Even you!" He poked me in the ribs and took out his guitar. "After that Charlie said he'd take us to Carlsbad Caverns!" He started tuning his guitar.

"You going to the lake?" Sarah had been talking with Liquid, leaning on the picnic table. "I'll come with you. I want to see what it looks like."

As we walked down the path, I heard Joey singing, "Sugar Magnolia, Blossoms blooming, heads all empty and I don't care…"

I didn't know if I wanted to do acid with Joey. The first couple of times I was really scared, not knowing what would happen. I had sex for the first time and didn't remember it! I had heard of kids going nuts, ending up in the hospital, unable to stop their trip, just going psycho. That's why I only took a third the first time and half the other times. My trips were pretty mellow so far. Lots of laughing, walls melting, hands trailing their images, colors, good music, fun people. Happy feelings.

The lake came up on us suddenly through a dark opening. It was huge. Brilliant sun reflected off boulders piled all the way down to the lake. Around the lake were groups of people swimming.

Sarah ran up to a big rock and motioned for me to come up. I stood next to her.

"This is beautiful."

We stood, taking in the scene.

"Hello, ladies." Jic stepped on the rock and Sarah jumped.

"Scared the shit out of me."

He laughed. "Beautiful, huh?"

We nodded.

"Going in?"

Sarah sat down on the rock. "Not me. I'm afraid of lakes. There are monsters on the bottom. Give me a pool any day."

I laughed. "I'm an ocean girl myself, but lakes are OK. I may go in. It's hot enough."

The sun was eleven o'clock high and beating down steamy hot. Must have been eighty-five already. Jic told us he had walked around and there were a lot of people but the place was so big you couldn't really tell. He said there were woods deep around us and a cliff you could climb and see some of the mountains in the distance.

"It's a really nice spot. We got lucky, since you guys have no idea where you are going."

"Joey says we'll go to Carlsbad Caverns. Charlie, a guy we met, will take us."

"Ah, sightseeing. Welcome to America."

I laughed and Sarah pointed to his jean shorts. "Aren't you hot?"

He had sweat on his face and there was a nice woodsy sweaty smell about him, not offensive, mostly rough.

He nodded. "Yeah, but I won't be in a minute. I'm going swimming."

He jumped the rocks down to the edge of the lake, landing on a big, flat boulder. Sarah motioned for me to sit next to her. As I did she raised her eyebrows and nodded to Jic.

We watched as Jic took off his tee shirt. Every detail flashed in my mind. Tan, muscles, strong back, and a tattoo of something on his right shoulder. He was facing the lake as he slipped off his sneakers, no socks.

"Here comes the party," Sarah chimed to me. "Don't let your eyes pop out."

We watched as Jic took off his jeans and kicked them aside. No underwear. His butt was tight with muscles all over. It looked like he spent his life running up and down mountains. You could see his tan line and his butt and legs were pale white. There was another tattoo on his left thigh, looked like some kind of snake.

He dove in and soon surfaced. "Hey! It's great! Come on in!" Then he swam away, strong, fast, arms cutting through the water.

"Wow." I sat on the rock. "Wow."

Sarah nudged me a few times. "You have a major crush on him. It is so obvious."

My eyes stayed on Jic. "Well, can you blame me? I mean, look at him. He's perfect."

She laughed. "Maybe for you."

"Nothing can happen, anyway. Remember, I'm with Joey."

"Yeah, well, we'll see." She took her hair in her hands. "I need to wash my hair badly. I can smell myself."

I turned from watching Jic in the water. "Are you gonna do that blotter acid that's around?"

She let go of her hair, shaking it out of her eyes. "Nah, that's not my thing. Too out of control. I was talking with

Liquid and he can get me some speed. I am so psyched. I can work on my paper in the cabin on the table by myself! When I get back to school, I will be ready for the start of the semester. I will just cruise! First, I have to think of the topic, of course, but no biggy. I have so many ideas!" She took a deep breath and smiled at me. "Are you?"

I shrugged and looked back at Jic, now treading water, looking up at us. I wonder if Jic would? Probably not. I hadn't seen him do any drugs on this trip, just drink a few beers.

"Maybe a half or something. It scares me a little."

"If you do, I'll take care of you. Speed makes you so in control. Except when you crash, that is." She was still touching her hair. "Feel how hard my hair is from being dirty." She pulled a bunch my way.

"Gross! I don't want to feel your nasty hair."

She pouted.

"I'll feel it after you wash it."

She stood up. "Can I leave you alone with lover boy?"

"Shut up! Course you can. Maybe."

She hugged me from behind and walked toward the path. I heard her yell, "Don't do anything I wouldn't do!"

I sat back down and felt Jic's eyes burning into me like the sun. I looked down at my knees and examined the long scratch on my thigh that had turned black.

"Lilly!" Jic was yelling from the water, motioning for me to come in.

I jumped the rocks down to the flat boulder where his clothes were. I was wearing short-shorts and a knit bikini top, and I wasn't going to take anything off. I couldn't dive, though.

Jic had swum near the edge. "It's OK. Jump. I'll catch you."

He grinned and held out his arms. His strong muscles were glistening with water, and my eyes moved down his body. The water was clear and I saw his strong thigh muscles treading water. I quickly looked away and then back, finding myself staring where I shouldn't be staring. He noticed and grinned wider.

I jumped in, almost on top of him. The water was freezing. I screamed.

He laughed. "You get used to it. Swim with me."

We swam together but I didn't stray far from the rocks. He stayed close and the fact that he was buck naked was on my mind the whole time.

"Don't you like to swim?" He splashed water at me and smiled.

I swam ahead, doing the breaststroke, the easiest one for me. "We spend every summer by the ocean at our beach house, so I only learned to ocean swim." I moved nearer to the rock, assessing whether it was close enough to save me from drowning.

"Ocean swimming is fun."

"How bout you?"

"On the swim team in high school."

I wondered how deep I was; I couldn't see the bottom even though it was clear.

"Yeah. Well, I'm heading to the rock. I need to be grounded."

He held out his arms. "I'll carry you."

"Really? I mean, no, it's OK." I felt hot like my head was going to blow off.

I climbed up and sensed he was getting out of the water also. If I turned around to stare it would be so obvious. If I hurried I could get to the rock first and then just naturally turn around to look at the lake and see him coming out of the water naked.

I got to the rock and turned around. He was facing the lake like before, and his pants were going over his butt. I watched him climb to me, sneakers and tee in his hand.

"Wow, that felt so good."

We both lay on the rock. The sun felt fantastic after all those damp days camping and freezing. It was burning hot and I loved the feeling. I looked through my fingers to see if there were any clouds. This was a game my sister and I would play on the beach; when there was a cloud, we would look carefully (because you could go permanently blind!) through our fingers and guess how many seconds until the sun came back out. When it did, it was such a reward. We would laugh and go back to our silent sun baking, just like Jic and I were doing. Why did she have to get sick? How was she? What was she doing on this day I was having so much fun? Well, I would call her today. Lu-Anne said we could use her phone and pay her at checkout.

"I want to call my sister today." My voice came out quiet.

"Good idea." Jic turned his head to me and we were facing each other.

"You need to call anyone? Your girlfriend or anything?"

Jic turned away and I felt hotter. Could I get any more obvious?

"My ex-girlfriend moved to LA. Question answered?"

"Just asking."

"Hey you guys!" Barry was at a different part of the lake and was waving to us. He had on checkered bathing suit shorts that were thigh high and baggy. His chest was all hair, and he had his glasses off. I wondered how he could see us. We both waved and watched as he dove in from a beach with no rocks. He swam and then yelled to us again. "Cookout at Charlie's! Hot dogs, burgers, everything!" He came out of the water and shook off his hair. "And Lilly, Joey wants you! Says he has a present!"

Jic nudged me. "Better go get your present."

I told him I was too sleepy to move. But I needed to call Jessie. So I stood up, feeling a little woozy from the sun. Jic said he would be along soon. I walked slowly through the woods. Didn't really want to leave the hot rocks with Jic. It felt like heaven.

I decided to go to the office first, before Joey. I walked through the campgrounds, passing some folks who were cooking lunch and who waved at me. When I reached the office, Lu-Anne was there, feeding a couple of cats and humming to herself. There was a smell of sweet bread baking from inside the cabin, and I wondered if this was her house. She had a big clock in the office, and I saw it was two fifteen. I think that was about four fifteen Boston time? Jessie should be off the beach and at the house.

When I asked about calling my sister, she held out her arm, ushering me inside.

"Sure, come on in." She brought me past the office into the back. There was a living room and a kitchen with another door that I guessed was her bedroom.

"Want some zucchini bread? With all these folks coming in, I'm baking it to sell! It's famous, you know. Lu-Anne's zucchini bread."

"I had a dream about it before I got here," I told her.

She handed me a warm piece of bread, thick with butter. I took a bite. Warm, sweet, soft—the best thing I had ever tasted.

"Wow!" I stared at her and she laughed.

"People travel miles for this. Watch how much traffic we get tomorrow on the Fourth. Mostly for the fireworks, but also for my bread!"

Lu-Anne sat me in a chair by her phone and went back into the kitchen. I really wanted another piece of zucchini bread with butter. I really didn't want to make this phone call.

As the phone rang at the beach house, I imagined what might be going on there. Everyone would be in from the beach, unless it was really hot there. My dad was away on business, so it was just my sister and mom.

The phone rang and rang. Usually my mom picked up after the first ring. I let it ring another ten times before hanging up.

I sat there staring at the wall. Pictures raced in my mind—my sister being rushed to the hospital again, intravenous tubes coming out of her arms to feed her, a broken down body. How could I know if she was OK?

Lu-Anne noticed me frozen and came over with another piece of bread. She handed it to me wordlessly and looked at my face, her eyes brimming with concern.

My appetite had gone but I didn't want to insult her, and she was looking at me with such care. I took a bite of warm bread and instantly felt better.

She smiled. "Everything OK?"

Should I tell her everything? Confide in her, let her be my friend, let her help me? I wonder what she would say. Maybe I would wait. Everything might be fine.

"No one answered."

Lu-Anne said I could call again any time she was in the office. She gave me a loaf to take back to our campsite. She didn't want any money. She gave me a big, bosomy incense-smelling hug and smiled at me with her missing teeth.

"Lilly, have a good time. You're on vacation, right? Have a good time." Then she led me out the door and disappeared back into the kitchen.

Walking back to the campsite, I thought about her and what she said. Have a good time. Really, I should. Why not? I didn't know how my sister was. Maybe she was at a party or hanging out with our summer gang. All the summers we went to the beach we would see the same kids. We would make bonfires at night, play Frisbee in the day, have mud fights, go bodysurfing, boogie boarding, and skim boarding. I kind of missed them, but I would see them in August. I would be back to my ocean, sand, waves, and beach friends.

By the time I got back to the neighboring campsite, lunch was in full swing. Joey was playing guitar with Liquid, Sarah was eating an ear of corn and doing some art thing with River on the picnic table, Sandy was sitting on Charlie's lap laughing, Barry had a bag of potato chips and was shoving them in his mouth with a beer at his side, another guy and his lady were by the grill tending to hot dogs and burgers, and even Jic was there, sitting against a tree with his hat pulled over his eyes, eating a hot dog.

I put the bread on the table by Sandy. "Lu-Anne gave this to us. It's amazing."

Sandy grabbed the bread and put it to her nose. "She gave you this bread? Wow. She must really like you. She never gives away this bread. It's famous, you know. People come from all over for it."

"So she said."

Sandy took Charlie's knife that he wore around his waist and began cutting up thin slices. She offered me, but I had two already. I wanted some real food.

Joey waved to me after he finished his song. "Where you been?"

He grabbed my face and gave me a wet kiss on the lips that smelled like hot dogs and relish. I wiped my mouth on my arm.

"Hey, I got you a present. I found it when I was exploring the cliffs. Look!"

From his back jeans pocket he pulled out a stick that was shaped like a cross. The bark was reddish and it looked like someone had carved it.

"Did you carve that?"

"No, that's the cool thing! I found it this way. Here, it's for you."

I took it even though he was the one that was obsessed with crosses.

"Thanks." I put it in my pocket. "Hey, I finally called my sister."

"Far out! Come on over here and listen to us play. This dude is good! Like Duane." Then he laughed really loudly and weirdly, and I knew that he was stoned.

"Did you drop that acid?"

He nodded. "I wanted to check it out! For Fourth of July! I'll probably just keep doing it and come down on the fifth of July!"

"Or at the end of July!" Liquid said, and they both laughed like hyenas. Joey started strumming again and it sounded awful.

I moved to the grill and got a burger. I looked around to see where to sit. Not by Joey, he was acting stupid. Sarah had finished eating and was taping things to a tree with River. Barry looked gross, chips all over his beard.

Jic was watching and our eyes met. He nodded his head. I walked over.

There was moss where he was sitting, a big patch, looking soft and green. I sat on it, really close to him.

"Sorry if I'm crowding you. I love moss."

"It's OK."

I bit into my burger that tasted amazing. It was like I hadn't eaten in days. I looked in the bun and saw bacon with cheese.

"This food is amazing. Lu-Anne gave me the best zucchini bread. It's over there; you should get some."

A loud bang made me jump until I saw that someone had joined Joey and Liquid with congas. Now people were coming from all over to jam with them and it was getting loud. There was a big woman with a bikini top and long skirt dancing to the music. She shouldn't have been wearing a bikini top, but I guessed she didn't mind the rolls of fat folding over everything.

"How did your call go? Is your sister OK?"

"Cool, but no one was home."

The big woman started belly dancing to the congas, and she was actually a great dancer. Some other adults joined her as well as three kids. The sweet smell of marijuana filled the air. Someone came over and handed me a jug of wine. I figured why not and took a swig. Then I asked them, "This isn't spiked with anything is it?" I didn't want to be tripping without preparation.

"No, man. We don't do that shit around here. Free choice." He offered the jug to Jic who shook his head. He flashed us a peace sign and went to pass the jug along.

I looked at Jic and giggled. He shook his head.

"Many characters around here, that's for sure." He picked up a stick and scratched the bottom on his bare foot with it.

I nodded. "By the way, what are your tattoos?"

Before he could answer, Sarah ran over to me, pulled me up, and brought me over to the dancing circle. She pushed me close to the belly dancing lady, who raised her hands and wiggled her belly for me.

Sarah screamed and said, "Do it, Lilly!"

Since I was wearing a halter and my belly was showing, I copied the belly dancer. Someone whistled and Sarah grabbed my hand, starting a dancing circle.

Wow. I was in the woods camping out in New Mexico with a bunch of hippies, dancing in a circle. How cliché. But it didn't feel cliché; it felt fun. Even Jic was laughing and smiling. Joey was strumming away, making awful music on the guitar, Barry had picked up a tambourine, and Sarah and I were dancing. The kids were running around, smells of food and smoke in the air, warm sun peeking low through the trees.

I stopped dancing and walked to the edge of the campground to take in the scene. The air smelled like the campfire, sweet with reefer and something like cookies. The sun was lower now. There must have been thirty people hanging out. Someone was playing a melodious flute with the drums. I watched Joey put down the guitar and go off somewhere with Liquid, Barry following. I wondered where they were going but didn't go after them. Joey was so high on acid I figured the other guys were taking care of him. Hopefully.

Worrying about Joey made me think of my sister. It must be getting toward nine back home. They should be home by now.

The woods were casting interesting shadows from the lowering sun. The smell of our party drifted with me as I made my way to the office.

I knocked on the door. Lu-Anne yelled, "Come on in!"

The house still smelled like zucchini bread and also incense. Lu-Anne was sitting on the couch with two large women. One of them was the belly dancer. There were lit candles everywhere. They had plates of food on the table: lasagna, vegetables, and some other stuff that I didn't recognize.

"Get a plate of food, honey, and pull up a chair. We're having women time."

The belly dancer laughed. "All time is women time."

They all laughed like it was the funniest joke in the world. I had no idea what they were talking about.

"Ah, I just need to use the phone again. No one was home last time."

Lu-Anne got up with difficulty, the woman on her left pushing her butt a little and all of them laughing again. It felt like a strange private party that I had no desire to join.

She walked me to the phone and went back. I watched her plop back down on the couch with the other women.

The phone rang and rang. No one picked up. I dialed the Newton house number. Again, there was no answer.

As I walked out Lu-Anne said, "Everything good?"

I nodded. No sense telling everyone my troubles.

Lu-Anne put her hand on the belly dancer's shoulder. "This is my woman, Cheri, or Cherry Pie, and over yonder is Betty. Sure you don't want to join us, honey? You look like you need some company."

I could use some company and it seemed friendly enough, but I didn't like the way Betty was looking at me smiling. And the cats were making my nose itch.

"Some other time," I managed to say as I walked out the screen door into the night.

Walking back my mind turned to Jessie. Was she OK? Did she go to the hospital again? Where was my mom?

It was getting dark and the music wafted through the trees. The smell of reefer and a cookout made me hungry for more food. I would forget about my family tonight and call them tomorrow. They were always at the beach house on July Fourth. I would call morning, noon, and night and get them on the phone. Everything would be all right.

The dancing had calmed down and everyone was sitting around the fire. I saw Sandy by a camper, the doors open, and she was putting a few kids into sleeping bags. The smoke from the fire smelled good and the light was calming.

Joey, Barry, and Sarah weren't around. I saw Jic on the picnic bench, whittling a stick and talking with Charlie, who was rolling a cigarette.

I sat down on the bench next to Jic.

"Where you been?"

"Called my sister, again. Didn't reach anyone in either house. Don't know what's going on; they should be there. I don't know. I'll call again tomorrow."

He looked at me deeply and nodded. I felt like I wanted to curl up in his lap, just an incredible wave of want spread throughout my whole being. I closed my eyes and breathed in.

"Here."

He was holding a Twinkie for me.

"I love these, where'd you get them?"

He nodded to the camper where Sandy and the kids were. "These guys are so generous. I want to buy all the food for tomorrow, at least, pitch in. We can go to town in the morning."

"Sounds good. Where is Sarah and everyone else? What time is it?"

"It's about nine. Sarah went back to the cabin to work on her paper. Joey and Barry went off to climb the cliff with Liquid. Joey was tripping his brains out and wanted to be on top of a cloud or something." Jic laughed and went back to whittling.

"What's your obsession with snakes? It looks like you're carving one."

Jic kept whittling. "I think they're cool. I have one on my leg, a tattoo, and may get another on the other leg. A different type."

"What's the other tattoo of, the one on your back?"

"Just something my ex-girl designed for me."

"How come you guys broke up?"

"She moved to California. To be in movies."

"Do you still love her?"

Jic stopped whittling and looked up at me.

"What? I'm just asking, that's all."

He shook his head and went back to his snake.

What? I was just asking. I have a boyfriend. Even though he's grossing me out. I don't want anything from Jic. Well, not much, anyway.

It was getting dark out and people were going back to their camps. Jic got up and said he was going to take a shower.

"Maybe I should wait for Joey to get back?"

He shrugged. "He's a big boy."

I walked back to the cabin with Jic. When we got there, Sarah was at the table writing furiously. She had a can of Tab and was tapping her foot as she wrote.

"Hi, you guys. I am on such a roll! Liquid gave me some speed, black beauties to be exact. I feel fantastic! This project is going to be great. I'm writing about Feminist Cooking Cooperatives and female-only events. Did you know there was a music festival this year in Michigan that didn't even allow boy children? Isn't that messed up? I want to explore the philosophy behind that, maybe interview the producers of the festival."

Jic interrupted. "Good night, girls, I'm going to bed."

Sarah's foot stopped tapping. "Hey, do you have any reefer? When I start to crash, I want it to be smooth."

"What?" I had never done speed, so I didn't understand.

She flipped her hair that was shining again from being washed. "Speed makes you feel great, really up. But when it starts to wear off, you feel grouchy and depressed. Smoking a joint helps you even out."

Oh. Sounded stupid to me. Take something to feel up, and then take something to go down? What's the point?

Jic didn't have any so he went to his room and closed the door. Suddenly I felt so tired from traveling, driving, everything. Like I hadn't slept in a week.

"Sarah, I'm going too." I kissed her cheek and she waved to me, her eyes darting madly at all the papers on the table.

Without even taking off my clothes, I put my head on the pillow. Considering how many people were at the campground, it was very quiet. I wondered again about Joey, then about Jessie. I told myself they were probably fine, and fell into the deepest sleep I had in days.

CHAPTER TEN

Into the Clouds

July Fourth! I woke up to the smell of bacon. Better than how I smelled. I hadn't showered in days. Now that I slept well, I would get clean and feel like a new person. The day was going to be busy.

I showered and used the strawberry-smelling shampoo and conditioner. There were clean towels piled up from who knows where, Sarah I suspected. She was crazy for clean.

I dressed in jean shorts and a paisley halter top, put a brush through my hair, and walked out of the bedroom.

Coming into the kitchen area, Sarah was busy at the stove cooking bacon and eggs. Jic was drinking coffee at the table reading a local paper.

Sarah turned around. She looked pale and strung out, her eyes glassy. She was chewing gum like mad.

"Breakfast? There's coffee, take some. I am too wired to eat; I need liquid for more speed to make it through this day and work more. Either that or I need to come down. What do you think? Oh don't answer. Are you hungry?

Sit down, have some food. You look good, Lilly. All fresh and rested. Doesn't she look good, Jic? She looks fresh and rested. I wish I was fresh and rested. I hate speed. I shouldn't do it. This is what always happens. I am so dumb, Lilly. I wish I was you."

I went over to Sarah and gave her a big hug. "It's OK. Go take a shower, you'll feel better. And then eat something!"

Sarah put all the food in the middle of the table.

"OK, you're right, I do need a shower." She took off her tee shirt right there in the kitchen. Her boobs were brown.

I had to laugh. "Sarah, how do you get your boobs tan?"

"I take my shirt off in the sun."

Jic was staring at Sarah's chest. He caught himself and turned, smiling. Sarah threw her tee shirt over a chair and walked into the bathroom, closing the door behind her.

I heard Jic take a deep breath. "Does she do that a lot?"

I laughed. "I don't know. Remember, I met her when you did?"

Jic shook his head. "OK. You should keep an eye on her today."

I attacked the bacon and eggs. They were delicious, all salty, buttery, and Sarah had put cheese in the eggs.

"Wow, this is so good! Where'd we get it?"

"I was up early and drove to town." Jic took out his cigarette paper and started rolling. He put tobacco on the paper and rolled it up with one hand. He made about ten cigarettes quickly. Then he put them in an empty pack of Camel non-filters. Taking out a matchstick from his flannel shirt pocket, he flicked it with his thumbnail and lit his cigarette.

I looked around. Everything was neat and I suspected that Sarah had stayed up all night, writing and cleaning. I wondered if Joey had made it back.

Footsteps answered my question. Joey stumbled into the kitchen from a bedroom, wearing boxers and a tee shirt. His Afro was wilder than usual, some of the curls going straight up and others in his eyes. He looked at me and Jic at the table and mumbled something like, 'Morning.' He went for the coffee pot, poured a cup, sat down on the wooden bench, put the cup up to his nose, closed his eyes, and seemed to fall asleep. When the cup was about to crash on the table, his head bobbed, which made his eyes pop open. He took a sip of the coffee and put it down.

Jic blew smoke rings. I walked around to Joey and sat next to him.

"You looked baked. What did you do last night, except tons of acid?"

His head moved slowly in my direction. His voice came out quiet and fuzzy. "Far out. It's really strong. Only do half. Or less. We did the cliffs. I did and Barry, Liquid followed. Beautiful birds. Fast. More today. Cliffs and acid. Ran into the dyke who runs the place. She was with her girlfriend."

"Lu-Anne? She's nice." I took another slice of bacon and offered one to Joey who shook his head.

"She hates men. Barry tried to get more cereal, even offered money, and she yelled at him, said to send the fast-talking blond or the brown-haired tan girl; that's you, Lilly. I think she has a crush."

Jic started laughing with Joey.

"What's so funny?" Barry came out in his jeans with his belly hanging over his pants. The only guy I know who can be on a road trip a week without eating much and get fatter.

Joey mumbled, "The muff-eater wants to muff eat Lilly."

Barry went into one of the shopping bags and pulled out some chips.

"Those are for Charlie, for the barbecue," Jic said.

Barry stuffed a handful in his mouth and put them back. He went to the stove and ate everything he could get his hands on that was still left, which was plenty. Sarah had cooked a lot.

There were loud bangs and popping outside our cabin and then laughter. Liquid was at the door with a sparkler, fire sparks flying everywhere.

"Rise and shine! Let's get this party going!" He came into the kitchen, waving the light stick around and laughing. Joey nodded his head, Jic watched the sparkler as it swirled by his head, and Barry pulled out a chair.

"Take a load off. You sleep?"

Liquid shook his head and said he was popping speed all night. He was going to sleep all day tomorrow, he said. For now, it was party time!

"Where's my girl Sarah? I have some beauties for her. Beautiful black beauties. Hey, man, you got another smoke?"

Jic took out the pack.

"Groovy, man. Hey we're gonna party today! Charlie's campground in an hour; he's handing out acid. Who's tripping, who's not?"

I raised my hand. "Not."

Jic said, "Not."

Barry shook his head.

Joey said, "Am. Continuing. To. Trip. Never came down. Going far to the clouds tonight, baby. Up to the mountaintop."

Barry poured some more coffee for Joey. "Just don't overdo it, OK bro? Someone should stay with you. How about you, Lilly? You are his girlfriend, after all. Remember that?" He gave me a dirty look, and I stuck out my tongue.

Joey put his hand up and started waving it. "Nah, it's not like that. We're cool. We're both free now. It's an open thing. Cool. Right, Lilly?"

I didn't remember having that conversation.

"We did? I mean sure, yeah, open thing is fine. I just don't remember talking about it, that's all."

Barry stood at the sink. "Actions speak louder than words."

I stared at him. "What's that supposed to mean?"

Joey waved his hand at Barry again. "Man, be cool. No freaking out, it's groovy." He reached over to me and gave me an open-mouth, big, wet kiss that smelled like stale beer and made me want to puke. I wiped my mouth on the back of my hand. Jic noticed and snickered. I stood up. This was getting all too close.

"I'm going for a swim. Hey, Sarah, want to come for a swim with me?" I went into the bathroom where she was putting on a sundress. "Come to the lake with me. Joey is getting weird and they're doing the guy laughing thing so I have to get out."

We walked out and Sarah saw Liquid. "Hey!"

Liquid whistled at her and looked her up and down. "You sure look fine!"

Sarah smiled and flirted her way beside him. "You have something for me?"

He rubbed against her. "I sure do!"

She slapped his arm playfully. "Not that! You know what I mean."

Liquid reached into his pocket and pulled out two pills. "How about these?"

Sarah was so excited she jumped up and down. "You got me more beauties! Thank you so much!" He handed them to her and she hugged him. He wouldn't let her go and she wriggled out of his arms.

There was an awkward silence. It was obvious what Liquid wanted in return, and I wasn't going to be the one to tell him differently.

Jic stood up. "I'll walk with you girls to the lake. Could use a swim too."

I pushed Sarah out the door as Liquid was patting her butt.

"Party starts soon at Charlie's. See you there, pretty girl. I'll look for your pretty flowered dress."

As we walked out, Sarah turned to me and made a face like she was sick.

"You totally led him on!" I grabbed her arm and turned to wait for Jic who was following us.

"I did not. I was just being friendly."

"She led him on, didn't she, Jic?"

Jic smiled. "Don't get me involved. But, yeah, ya did."

"Well, I got what I wanted." Sarah patted her pocket.

"Slut!" I pushed her with my hip. Then I got serious. "Maybe you should cool off those things. You get so wired and whatnot."

"That's the whole point! But I know what you mean. These will be my last ones."

We walked through the woods down the path. It must have been about noon, the morning had passed so quickly. It was hot already. I remembered something and stopped.

"Shoot, I have to call my sister. They haven't been home and it's weird."

Sarah took my arm. "Let's swim first. There's plenty of time."

That was true and if something was wrong, I didn't want the whole day to be ruined. Maybe I would call tomorrow, after July Fourth and all the festivities. A day wouldn't matter.

The lake was sparkling and there were a lot of people already swimming. Sarah would only go up to her knees so we went to the beach (at that level she could maintain control of all the underwater monsters). By the edge of the water, there was an older woman with a long, white braid, tan face, and a kind smile. She was holding hands with a small girl as the girl was jumping in the water. She looked up at us and nodded.

Jic said, "That's Miriam," and walked over to the woman.

I felt drawn to follow Jic and did so. Sarah was busy checking for fish by her feet. When I got to the woman, she smiled warmly and Jic introduced her.

I smiled at the pretty little girl who was digging a hole close to the woman's leg.

"Are you staying for the party today? There's one at Charlie's campsite not far from here. Everyone is invited if you and your daughter want to come."

"Oh no, we live in a cabin a few miles from this campground. My granddaughter, Cane, enjoys the lake and seeing all the people coming in for the Fourth. We'll come back tonight to see the fireworks."

Sarah screamed and jumped out of the water. "A fish bit me!" She sat on the sand and started inspecting her toes. Cane ran over to her and looked in the water, wanting to see fish.

"They're just tiny minnows, look." She pointed and we all looked at a school of small, innocent-looking fish. She patted Sarah on the head. "They're not dangerous. You don't have to be afraid."

Sarah looked up at her. "What a sweet girl you are."

Cane pointed. "If you watch them, you won't be so scared."

Miriam walked over and took Cane's hand. "We have to get going to our barbecue; maybe we will see everyone later at the fireworks. People usually congregate here since the best view is over the lake and up by the cliffs." She pointed to the other side of the lake where there were steep rocks to the right. "They usually light them right over there. Beautiful, colors galore, looks like a magic show." She looked into my eyes. "All your worries just go up in smoke."

I watched as Miriam and Cane walked up the path. Cane turned around and looked at us before disappearing into the woods.

How does she know I have worries? Who was she? Why is she leaving so fast?

Sarah was still inspecting her feet. "Even though she said they were minnows, I think something bit me."

I turned to Jic who was looking out to the cliffs.

"Cool people. Where'd you meet them?"

He didn't answer for a while.

"What are you looking at?"

He shook his head. "Nothing. Just thinking about Joey on those cliffs last night. They are really steep and he was pretty baked."

He turned to me. "Miriam was here yesterday collecting rose hips in the woods. We spoke for a while. She's really interesting, born and raised around here."

Behind us in the woods we heard a huge explosion of firecrackers. It made me jump. Liquid, Joey, and another guy I didn't recognize came laughing out of the woods. Liquid was carrying a bottle of wine and seemed loaded already.

"Party time, girls and boys! Come on down! Here, have some wine, have a fine time, dance until nine!" He came over and put his arm around Sarah. He attempted to kiss her and she pulled away.

"Look, I know you gave me some speed and I appreciate it. But I'm a lesbian!" She said this so loudly Jic and I started laughing.

This didn't seem to phase Liquid, who moved toward her again. "That's cool, I like girl-on-girl."

Sarah shook her head and moved over to me. "Guys don't take a hint, do they?"

"That wasn't a hint!"

Joey held open his hand. I went over and it was the blotter acid. There were two squares of it.

"Who wants some? Remember, it's strong!" He took a square and popped it in his mouth.

"Joey! You said it was strong! And half is good enough!" I glared at him.

He shrugged. "Yeah, but I'm immune since I did it yesterday. I can handle at least a whole hit. You, on the other hand, should take just a quarter!" He ripped a piece off the one that was left and put it on his finger.

"Open up!"

I shook my head. "No, I'm good. None for me."

"Come on! Trip with me, baby." He moved his body close to mine and I felt him press into my leg. He whispered, "We can spend some time in the woods. Umm. You're still my girl, after all."

The others had started up the path to the party. Sarah looked back at me like she was wondering if I needed her. I shook my head and she disappeared into the woods.

I looked at Joey's already stoned-out face. He looked disgusting. Glassy eyes that wouldn't focus, tongue moving over his lips that were wet like he couldn't feel his spit, his face all red and flushed.

"I'm not your girl anymore. Remember? You're the one who said it in the cabin. Free, remember?"

He moved away from me. "Yeah, you're right. Forget it."

"Are you mad?"

"No, course not. Far-out." He popped the quarter acid in his mouth. "Let's go to the party."

"Joey!"

He walked away into the woods. I couldn't believe he had taken more acid.

The party was in full swing. It had stretched out to the surrounding campsites, with three fires going, grills cooking food, musicians jamming, kids running around. People were smoking pot, drinking wine, eating food, laughing, hugging, kissing, and chasing kids.

A wave of despair came over me. I didn't want to be here. I couldn't see Jic or Sarah. These strangers were dancing around, stoned and smiling. There was a circle of hippies with their eyes closed. Where were other teenagers? Everyone seemed too old or too young. Where were Sarah and Jic? I wanted my sister and my friends from school.

A guy with long, blond hair came up to me and took my hand. "Smile, sister, everything is groovy!"

I felt like hitting this happy hippie. I forced a fake smile, moved my body like I was dancing with him, and then took off in the other direction, through the woods, running to Lu-Anne's office.

"Honey, what's wrong?" Lu-Anne was in the kitchen as I came in. She was stirring a big pot of something chili-like. There was the smell of cornbread coming from the oven.

Her girlfriend Cheri was there too, sitting on a stool. "Honey, what is it? You look freaked out."

I leaned on the counter and everything spilled out. "There are so many people at the campsite, dancing, singing, and happy together. What's wrong with me? I feel so…out of it. Just a big disconnect. I'm so worried about my sister. Where is she? Why doesn't my mom answer the phone? What if my sister is in the hospital again? What if my mom can't handle it? What if my dad doesn't come back from his business trip? They don't know where to reach me! The last time we spoke was like a week ago.

What if something really bad happened and I don't know about it!"

Lu-Anne handed me a cup of tea that smelled like dirty socks. "Here, drink this chamomile tea, it will calm you."

I took the tea and sat next to Cheri. Lu-Anne stirred the pot and then faced me. "What if my house catches fire? What if my hair falls out? What if my cornbread is bad?"

Cheri put her hand on mine. "What if Lu-Anne decides she doesn't want me anymore? What if—the sky falls? The stars go out?"

"What we are saying, Lilly is that you can't live like that, fearing what might happen next. It never goes down like you think. There's no point in 'what if.' You can't worry so much. How old are you?"

I sipped the tea. It wasn't as bad as it smelled. "Almost sixteen."

Lu-Anne took the cornbread out of the oven. There were six beautiful loaves that smelled like heaven. She wrapped one in a kitchen towel and handed it to me.

"Go eat this with some of your friends. Relax! You'll reach your family. Try again tomorrow. Don't worry so much! Learn that lesson now and you will be much better off."

Joey was with the musicians, tripping his brains out, looking up at the sky. He was enjoying the beat beat beat of his thoughts as they made a pattern with colors, in his brain:

It smells like blue, I taste it! To the cliff. Edge birds. Quick! I, the strongest, the secrets of the woods. Save the clan, my destiny, only then I am redeemed.

Joey sat rocking his body to the music and watching the colors floating around his eyes.

I walked out of Lu-Anne's cabin feeling better. The bread was warm against my stomach and talking had helped.

The party was in full swing. More people had arrived and the musicians were jamming with guitars, banjos, tambourines, and drums. Kids were running around. I put the bread on the table, sat on the bench, cut a piece to eat, and looked around for Jic and Sarah.

I heard Joey before I saw him. His voice was going low to high and was creepy.

"Lilly, dance with me! Lilly, where are you?" Joey was leaning against a tree near where the musicians were. I looked over.

He saw me at the same time and stumbled sideways to me. He had to hang on to each tree for balance. When he got to me, I sat him down. He smelled like some kind of alcohol. His eyes were glassy and he looked so high. His nose was running and he smelled. I noticed his face glistening with sweat.

"I love you, I love the rocks, trees, the mission, it's all there!" He tried to stand up but wobbled. "Come with me!" He pointed to the sky.

I grabbed his arm and sat him down.

"Joey, you're not going anywhere. You are way too high. Just stay here with us so we can watch you. What else did you do?"

Joey wrestled out of my grip. "Two, three, four, and five. The woods, Lilly! Fly... it's amazing!" His voice disappeared as he stood quickly, dancing toward the fire, laughing to himself. I ran after him but Liquid, who was playing a harmonica, got to him first, before he fell into the flames.

"I got him!" Liquid grabbed his arm and led him to the musicians. "Come play your guitar, man."

"Yeah, man, that's great. We are flying! Lilly is my woman!"

He was so embarrassing; it was hard to be with him. Spit was coming from the side of his mouth. I was glad Liquid was there to hang with him. Barry should be there too.

I looked around and saw Barry across the fire pit talking with Charlie and Sandy.

I yelled over the music to Liquid. "You got him?" Liquid gave me the peace sign, and I ran over to talk with Barry.

Sandy gave me a pretty smile. "What's wrong, sugar?"

They were hanging by their camper, and I saw the kids in sleeping bags eating cookies. They looked so sweet and simple.

"Joey is way too stoned. He did a bunch of acid and has been drinking too. He's talking about flying and some other garbage. Barry, can you stay with him?"

Barry sneered at me. "I'm not his father. He is seventeen, ya know."

"Yeah, but he's just way too high! He's talking and acting crazy!"

Barry looked over at Joey in the group of musicians. "You take care of him then. He's your boyfriend. Or, he was before you dumped him for Jic. So you play mommy for a change."

"I didn't dump him for Jic!"

"Yeah, whatever." We stood in silence. Sandy smoothed my hair and said she could help after putting the kids to bed.

Charlie shook his head. "Man, he didn't listen to me. I didn't want anyone having a bad trip. It's strong stuff; I told him to take half. I'll go over, see if he will hang in his cabin until it wears off." Charlie walked across to the musician's corner and Sandy went in with the kids. That left Barry and me staring at the ground.

I really didn't want to hear Joey talking about love, flying, and other crazy things. It looked like I had no choice, though.

"I'll go too." I started to walk away and Barry grabbed my arm.

"No, I'll go; I'm going to smack him sober. He does this to me all the time. He won't do it again, I'll tell you that."

Barry walked across to him. I walked closer to the fire where I could see them. It was warm and the wood smelled so good. I saw Jic out of the corner of my eye.

"Hey, Jic, where you been?"

He had a hamburger in his hand. "There's a quieter party next door, more my style. Better food too! Want a bite?"

I shook my head and nodded to Joey. "We are all watching Joey. He's severely fucked up."

"He did seem too excited about that acid. I hear it's really strong."

"He's an idiot. He's also been drinking."

"Bad combination."

"I know. And he's talking crazy about flying off cliffs!"

Jic finished his burger. "It's a good thing Barry and Liquid are with him. Although Liquid won't be much help; he's so high on speed and whatever."

I looked at Jic in the firelight. He was tan from the day, had his hair tied back, and his legs had dirt on them. He smelled like trees. I wanted to touch his face, feel his muscles, so much more. I looked back into the fire. What a time to be thinking like that! I was glad my face was hidden in the shadows.

Jic rolled his neck around and stretched. He picked up a stick and threw it into the fire. "I hate drugs. In the city, New York, that is, there's this great place to hear music, the Fillmore East. Allman Brothers, the Dead, Earth Wind and Fire, everyone plays there. Before I went to North Carolina, I'd go every week. A lot of the folks drink and do drugs all the time. They make fools of themselves, taking off their clothes, dancing on stage, and falling down. What a stupid waste of time. They don't even hear the music! I like to be able to remember what I did. I went with a friend who did acid and was drinking Jack Daniel's. He didn't remember anything, and he got sick on the train ride home. It was disgusting. What's the point of that? The people around you have to take care of you, and they end up hating you. Big waste of time."

I stared at him.

"What?"

"You haven't talked that much this whole trip."

He looked straight at me. "Most of the time, I don't have much to say."

"I like hearing you talk."

Joey was sitting on the bench, hallucinating.

Wow. What is this world? Red, yellow, blue, smells like it's on fire, blazing, no one is invisible. What was that? Bleep. Mind surgery.

Joey stood up and said loudly, "I have to piss." Barry stood up to go with him, but Joey pushed him away and ran into the woods.

I poked Jic. "There goes Joey."

Jic and I ran over as Barry ran after him, yelling.

I noticed people were leaving the campsite walking down to the lake.

"Hey, fireworks time!" Liquid turned and ran down the path. So much for watching Joey.

"Jic, should we go into the woods? Or wait for them here?"

The campsite was quiet now. We waited a couple of minutes and when nothing happened, we went down to the lake, seeing if they were there.

People were gathered around and I could feel their excitement. Jic and I stood in the back of the crowd looking around. There were little kids sitting on blankets waving around sparklers. The adults were laughing and waiting for the show.

I couldn't see Joey or Barry. There were too many people. I didn't feel like being in this crowd. Everyone was way too cheery. And I was scared.

I saw Barry running out of the woods onto the beach, stopping and talking with people. He looked tense. Joey was not with him. He spotted us and ran over.

"Did Joey come down here?" He looked frantic.

My breath stopped. "I thought you were with him."

"I was. He went to take a piss, then he was gone, in like, two seconds."

Jic put his hand on Barry's shoulder. "We saw you go after him. You did the right thing, man. You tried to follow him."

Barry looked up. "I have to go to the cliffs. He was talking about them all day."

I remembered that. He wanted to fly, high in the sky. "Barry, maybe he's with Sarah. I haven't seen her all night."

Barry shook his head. "Sarah's in the cabin."

We heard explosions come from the woods and then laughter. We all turned, hoping Joey would walk out. It was another bunch of people walking to the beach.

Then came the first fireworks. They were so loud I had to cover my ears. Everyone clapped, which was even louder.

"I'm going to the cliffs." Barry walked away just as Liquid showed up. He was carrying a huge flashlight. He seemed to have sobered up and was walking in a straight line. Charlie was with him, eyes darting all around.

Liquid said something I didn't hear, and the three of them ran across the beach to the path that led around the lake.

Which left Jic and me standing there. Fireworks started going off all over the place. Bright colors, noisy bangs that seemed to explode right inside my head. Shut up! We have to hear Joey, we have to see him, please, turn off the noise! Why did he have to do this?

"More, more!" The kids were yelling and laughing, jumping up and down. I wanted to run up the cliff myself;

I wanted to stop the fireworks. What was going on? Bang, crash, more noise!

I put my hands over my ears. Jic was standing there motionless, watching the cliff. I leaned into him as we watched and waited. Every new explosion tore through me. Then the sky seemed to light up in silence.

My eyes closed as I uttered a prayer. *Please, God wherever you are and whoever you are, help Joey!*

I couldn't stand there any longer. I had to help find him.

"Jic, come on! We have to look." I grabbed his hand and we ran away from the laughing and cheering into the dark forest. Running along the path, he let go of my hand and we took off fast. The explosions were even louder in the woods, echoing off the trees. We were moving closer to the firing station. Maybe Joey was watching. Laughing and having a good time.

There was a clearing and then a path that went straight up to the cliff. We stopped. There were Barry and Liquid, starting to climb up the treacherous path. The top must have been over fifty feet above.

I screamed, "Where are you going?"

Barry leaned against a tree and turned to us. "We saw him go this way, we think. Or that way," he pointed. He turned and climbed after Liquid.

"This way." Jic and I continued along the lake path. The fireworks were so loud that we smelled the smoke they were so close, the colors were exploding in our eyes, and moving closer was awful but Joey could be there. Around the bend, any minute we could see him. It wasn't that long since I saw him last. How far could he be?

We raced along. The path ended with a bunch of fallen branches and brush. Above us was the cliff with no way to climb. It was a dead end.

And I didn't see Joey anywhere.

My heart was coming out of my chest. Sweat was pouring down my arms, and everything blurred together from the darkness and my tears.

Then I saw the shadow from above. A movement.

"Jic!" I pointed and he saw.

It was so far up, the shadow.

"Joey!" I yelled at the top of my lungs. "Jic, it can't be him! I can't see, can you? Joey! Hey!"

There was no movement. The shadow stood about ten feet from the edge.

"Lilly, he won't hear us."

"Can you tell? Is it him? JOEY!"

I climbed over the fallen branches to get closer. Maybe I could climb fast; maybe there was a way. Trees and brush scratched at my bare legs, stinging them. I didn't care. Get closer.

"Lilly, there's no way!"

The fireworks stopped. They were getting ready for the finale. The air was thick with smoke. And then, something else. It was his voice. Joey was shouting, no, he was singing! I couldn't hear words, but I knew it was him!

"Jic! It's him! Come on, let's get him!"

The fireworks started again; this time the blasts lasted forever. I covered my eyes, the brightness stinging them. I felt something warm and wet dripping down my leg. In the light I saw it was blood from a big, open scratch. I wiped it with my hand.

Again, silence hit me like a bullet. The sky darkened. No more blasts, no more singing, nothing.

The shadow was barely visible and it was moving. Slowly. To the edge. I ran, into more brush. Jic climbed over some trees behind me. The shadow raised his arms like a bird.

"No!" My scream caught in the wind, echoing back at me, mocking.

My arms flew up on their own, as if to catch him. He was in the air. He had pushed himself off the cliff. I kept running forward and there were more trees blocking me. Then I froze.

Faster than air, he disappeared.

I fell and all was still.

Jic ran over. He knelt beside me on the leaves.

"Hey. Hey."

I was so dizzy. My stomach was in my throat, and I thought I would be sick. Jic put his hand on me.

"Jic." I could barely breathe. "We have to go to him." My legs were stinging in pain. In the moonlight I saw scratches, dried blood, dirt.

I turned to Jic and hoped in his eyes I would see that it wasn't real. What I saw was panic.

Then we heard sirens and watched, motionless as off-road vehicles tore through the woods, red lights flashing. What were they doing?

Maybe it wasn't Joey. The fireworks had been so loud, Barry and Liquid were climbing to find him. It was an animal, or a fallen tree. It couldn't be Joey.

My legs were immobile. Jic was standing by me. I kept hearing Joey's voice singing. Maybe he was coming down now, climbing down the path. My head was exploding. The scratches were stinging, and streaks of blood were drying up and down my calves and knees.

Jic pulled me up and we began walking. My eyes were blurred, and I didn't know where we were going. I kept hearing Joey's voice singing. My head was exploding.

And then we were back in our cabin, the bright lights stinging me.

Jic sat me down and took a wet cloth to my legs.

I pushed my legs away. "I don't care! I'm OK, we have to find Joey!"

The door swung open. Liquid stumbled in and collapsed on the floor. His face was tear-stained and tight. I couldn't look at him, and every time I closed my eyes, all I saw was the shadow going down, down and the awful echo.

Liquid put his head in his hands and made terrible moaning sounds. Shut up, please, I thought. Then he started to talk in a shaky, high voice surrounded by tears.

"Barry, he went in the ambulance."

I winced at a deep scratch that Jic was cleaning. "What ambulance?"

Jic and Liquid stared at me.

"What?"

Liquid shook his head. "Man, Joey is gone, that's the whole thing, he's gone!" He put his head in his hands and started that moaning again.

"Shut up!" I wanted to run but my legs felt so heavy. And Jic was washing them. His eyes were caring and his hands were touching me.

Sarah came out of the bedroom, in her tee shirt, looking sleepy. When she saw us her eyes widened. "What happened?"

No one said anything.

"Lilly? Jic? What is going on?"

From the floor, in his broken voice, Liquid said, "Joey. He jumped. Off the cliff."

Sarah leaned against the sink and looked down at my torn-up legs. "I don't understand."

Jic looked at her intensely. "Sarah, Joey did too much acid and thought he could fly. He jumped off the cliff. He's on his way to the hospital."

Sarah's mouth fell open. "Is he…dead?"

I jumped up and the bloody cloths fell off my legs. "Course not! We don't even know it was him! He'll just walk in here with Barry any minute. We don't know anything." My legs hurt so much. I sat back in the chair.

Sarah knelt next to Jic. "Look at your legs!" She picked up the cloth that Jic had put down and washed off more dirt and blood. The scratches were long and one was still bleeding.

The door swung open. I looked up, hoping it was Barry and Joey.

It was Lu-Anne. She had a thermos and cups.

She didn't say anything, just poured us something minty-smelling. "Drink the tea."

We all picked up the cups. What was she doing?

"Barry called me. He's at the hospital." She took a deep breath.

I pushed my cup away. "Barry is looking for Joey, they're in the woods. You have it wrong. You weren't even there. Joey disappeared, and Barry found him, and…"

"Lilly!"

She scared me with the sharpness of her voice and I stopped.

Lu-Anne started again. "Lilly. Joey is dead."

No one spoke.

"He died instantly from the fall."

Sarah choked a word out. "Fall?"

She cleared her throat. "The jump. They said he died instantly."

Jump. Flailing arms. Shadow falling. Echoes. It was Joey. Dead. Joey dead. Instant death. He jumped. Could it be that simple?

Jic put down the rag and stared at the floor. Sarah put her hands across her eyes. Liquid stayed on the floor and started that horrible moaning sound.

I couldn't hear that sound, any sound, no more. No more noise. I stood up and went into the bedroom and lay down. Finally it was quiet. No need to wake up from this awful dream; another one would come soon. They always did. First a nightmare, then the happy dreams. Closing my eyes all I could see was the dark sky. The outline of a body. A black Afro. I remember the first time I saw that black Afro on that white boy. The sparkle in his brown eyes. His full, soft lips, that first kiss. His woodsy smell, his excitement, his love. His wanting me. Wanting me to be with him, wanting me so much we went on this road trip, this California trip where everything fell apart, everything went wrong, and he was gone.

I wanted to reverse the clock. Go back to the lake, the crystal sparkling lake when we were just falling in love.

In the quiet I heard him singing. He was back! This was a dream!

"Joey?" I yelled louder so he could hear me. "Joey?"

Sarah and Jic came running in, sitting on the bed next to me, hugging me.

"Joey?" I looked at their faces.

Then the tears came, all of us, we sat there sobbing, we lay there sobbing. We fell asleep sobbing.

The morning sun woke us up.

CHAPTER ELEVEN

Memories by the Fire

There was yellow in the back of my eyelids. But they wouldn't open. They were glued together. I rolled to my side.

There was Sarah, on the edge of the bed, staring out the window.

I touched her back. "Is it true?"

She nodded and stroked my hair. "I hoped it was a dream too."

I looked at the ceiling. "Where's Jic?"

"He went to pack the car."

I felt panic. "He's leaving?"

"All of us are."

I looked up at her bright green eyes. "Sarah, this was all my fault. He asked me to be with him after he took the first bunch of acid. I said I didn't want to, he said OK, and then took more acid! If I had said yes, he wouldn't have taken more, he would still be alive!"

Jic came in the room. He came over to me and looked at my legs. He opened a tube that was in his hands.

"This will help heal your scratches." His eyes met mine and I felt giddy and then guilty and then weird. He applied the cream and stood up. "That will help." He walked out.

I whispered to Sarah, "And my feelings for Jic. Joey could tell! But we didn't do anything, nothing happened." I felt like tearing at my legs and making them bleed again. What was wrong with me? My boyfriend just flew off a cliff, and I wanted to wrap my body around another guy.

"Lilly. Listen. You are not to blame. He did too much acid. If you were together, he may have taken more. You don't know. You can't control another person. And you can't cause them to jump off a cliff! In Austin, he was so baked. And Barry told you he did too much, right? Don't you dare blame yourself. I could blame myself too. I was a speed freak this summer. Not anymore, though. I don't care if I ever see another hit of speed in my life."

"Yeah, but what if I was a better girlfriend?"

"What if he was a better boyfriend? What if he didn't do drugs or drink? What about that? So don't go there. OK?"

Just like Lu-Anne and her girlfriend had told me.

She took my head in her hands and looked me straight in the eyes. "Promise. Neither of us blame ourselves."

I nodded.

We walked out of the bedroom into the kitchen. All of our supplies were on the kitchen table. Clothes, blankets, sleeping bags. Jic and Liquid were shoving everything into the car.

I didn't know what to do. Sarah took my hand and we went to the bedroom to put clothes in our backpacks. Joey's flannel shirt was on the floor. I picked it up and held it to my nose. The smell of him overwhelmed me. Woodsy, sweet, and smoky. Just like I remember him back in Newton by the lake. Before…all of this.

I put on the shirt and left the room.

I stood in the kitchen, looking out the window. The car was full and the cabin almost empty. It felt all wrong. Joey was supposed to be with us when we left the campground. We were going to Carlsbad Caverns today. We hadn't seen any sights of America yet. How could we be going home? I didn't want to leave this place, the last place he was alive.

Sarah and Jic were at the car when Sandy and Charlie came. I walked out and heard Jic talking. He was going to drive us to the airport; we would meet Barry there. Jic would drive the Volkswagen back East and meet us in Boston. By Sunday. In time for Joey's funeral.

Sarah put out her arm and I leaned against her. I had never felt so tired. "We have to do something for Joey. A memorial. Here, not back home."

Sarah nodded. "We were talking about that."

Jic said, "We don't have a lot of time. Joey's parents want him and Barry home by tomorrow. They can't bury him on Friday because it's the Sabbath, they're Jewish, so it will be Sunday."

Charlie gave him a light. "Hey, man, how will you drive to Boston by Sunday?"

Jic didn't say anything.

"Man, Sandy and I can give you some food so you don't have to stop."

Sandy, in her soft voice, said, "What about a simple memorial fire at our campsite? He spent some sweet good time there playing with the musicians. He looked happy there."

"Barry should be at it." I wanted to call him to be there, to come back from the hospital. What does someone do at a hospital once the person they are visiting dies?

I guess they leave because Barry walked up just as I thought that. He looked thinner, his face drawn out and pale. He had last night's clothes on.

Everyone took turns hugging him. His eyes were full and he wiped tears away. When he looked at me I felt afraid. Does he think it's my fault?

All the anger that he seemed to carry the whole trip was wiped out of him. He came over and gave me a big hug.

"I'm sorry," I whispered in his ear.

He nodded. "Me too."

We told Barry our plans. He went to the cabin to take a shower, grabbing some clothes and towels that we had packed. We all went to Sandy and Charlie's campsite to start the fire.

Sandy's children were running around, innocently making mud pies. It was strange, seeing life go on as usual. Sandy put on some Grateful Dead music, which was Joey's favorite band. Liquid came out from the campsite next door. He looked different. His hair was combed back, his face was clean, his eyes sad and his face drawn.

Jic, Sarah, Sandy, Charlie, Liquid, and I stood around the fire that had lit quickly from last night's embers. Joey was by that same fire last night, talking with me, laughing. I wished he hadn't been so high, I wished his nose hadn't been running, he wasn't drooling, I wished he didn't take those drugs and drink, I wished he was standing with us to say good-bye, and say hello to the next stage of our road trip.

Barry joined us and we stood quietly. The air smelled like woodsy smoke, and I kept thinking of how excited Joey was about this road trip.

"Joey talked about this road trip from the first time I met him. He was so happy and excited. It was all he talked about."

Barry nodded his head. "That's all he wanted, to make it to California. To play the guitar. To be happy. My little brother." I think he wanted to say more, but his voice cracked and he put his head down. Charlie put his arm around him, as did Liquid, who was on the other side.

"He was my brother, and I can't believe he's not here."

We stood for a while longer looking at the fire. Without speaking, Charlie stepped up to the fire, put a stick in, and said, "This stick symbolizes the guitar Joey loved to play when we were jamming. Joey, keep jamming, wherever you are." We watched it burn and crackle.

Liquid stepped forward. He had a rock in his hand that he held up. "Joey, this is for how much you loved rock and roll." He tossed the rock into the fire.

Sarah walked slowly toward the fire holding a tree branch with lots of green leaves. "Joey loved talking with people. He was really friendly. This represents all the people who Joey made happy."

Barry took our road map out of his pocket. He unfolded it and the map fluttered in his hand. "Joey wanted this road trip so badly. He loved to see new places." He threw the map in the fire and we watched it burn. "I hope he's taking the best road trip of his life." He put his head down.

I had on the same jean skirt from last night. I dug into my pocket and took out the cross that Joey had given me.

I couldn't help smiling as I remembered how excited he was when he gave it to me. "Even though Joey was Jewish, he was interested in all religions and had a fascination with crosses. He found this the first time he went to the cliff. He said it was a treasure from the cliff. I'm giving it back to him and hope he keeps looking for treasures, wherever he is."

I threw it in the fire. It crackled as it burned.

Jic was last and had something in the palm of his hand that he held up. It was an Oreo cookie. "I've never seen anyone eat Oreos the way Joey did. He would take all the insides out, make a ball of sugar, eat it, then pile the chocolate pieces up and stuff those in his mouth. He looked so happy eating them. I think he went through ten bags of Oreos in the past week."

Jic threw the Oreo in the fire. "Joey, wherever you are, I know you're eating Oreos."

We stood together, the smoke swirling around us.

The wind blew cool, fresh air. Woodsy smells filled my nose as I breathed deep, looking around for the last time.

Barry put out his hand to Charlie. "Time to go, man. Thanks for all your help, your love. You guys are famous, man."

They hugged and then everyone was hugging. Charlie, Sandy, and Liquid walked us to the car. We piled in.

I couldn't believe we were leaving. We waved good-bye and rode down the dirt path.

Lu-Anne was sitting outside on her chair. She put her hand up and came over to the car. She handed us a bag of food: sandwiches, candy bars, juice. And of course two loaves of her homemade zucchini bread, still warm from the oven.

Every step, every good-bye felt like a dream. I wanted to be asleep. I couldn't wait to get on the airplane.

Barry drove to the airport, twenty minutes away. We listened to a country station and didn't say much. The fire smell was on our clothes, and when I closed my eyes, I was still at the campfire.

The next good-bye was to Jic. I wanted him to stay, wanted his strong arms around me, wanted to lean on his shoulder, wanted him near me like he'd been the past seven days. He hugged me so tightly and whispered in my ear. "I'll see you in a few days."

I whispered back, "I want to go with you. Let's drive west, keep going, this is too intense."

He pulled away and looked deeply into my eyes. He took my hand and then walked away, getting into the car with one last nod of his head to everyone. We watched him drive off.

Barry went into business mode. We got our tickets and went straight to the gate. Soon we were in our seats waiting for the plane to take off to Logan Airport, Boston. Barry by the window with Joey's guitar at his feet, Sarah in the middle, and me on the aisle.

I didn't want to think anymore. But my mind had other ideas. I hadn't spoken to my parents in days, didn't know what was going on with my sister, wondered if they knew anything about what was going on. Joey's parents were flying in from Europe to bury their youngest son. It felt so unreal. Where would I go tonight? To the beach house? With Barry? How would I explain? "Hi, Mom, this is my friend Sarah. We're home early 'cause Joey was on acid and thought he could fly and ended up killing himself. How's everything with you?" It was too much to even think about. I put the earphones on and drifted as the plane took off. Jic was driving on the road below us, listening to a country tune, smoking, and eating Milk Duds. I wished I were wrapped around his body. Hightailing it to California.

CHAPTER TWELVE

Beach House

My mother and sister met us at the airport with Joey's father. Joey's dad, a taller replica of Joey, with shorter hair and a businesslike air, whisked Barry off with just one glance at Sarah and me.

My sister hugged me so tightly. She felt better, not like a skeleton. My mom was as tense as I'd ever seen her. Driving to the beach house was awful—Sarah in the back with my sister and my mother with her monologue in the front seat. Couldn't she see that we'd just lost our good friend?

"I didn't hear from you and then I get this call from some woman called Lu-Anne…"

I had to smile and looked back at Sarah who was smiling too.

Jessie whispered to Sarah, "Who?"

I heard Sarah describing Lu-Anne to Jessie as my mother went on and on.

"She says Joey, your boyfriend, who I don't even know, he was on this trip with you? That Joey jumped off a cliff? I mean, who jumps off a cliff? She goes on to say that you are flying home. Who paid for your airfare? Then we have to leave the beach house today; it's a beautiful beach day, the traffic was terrible, and Jessie isn't feeling well…"

"Mom, I'm feeling fine. It's OK."

Jessie did look better. She had a tan and her eyes were bright. She looked pretty.

"Your father is at an insurance conference in New Jersey; he has been gone most of the summer and I've been stuck by myself at the beach house. Not that it's been bad; I have a lot of friends at the beach, one in particular…" my mother giggled in a way that made my stomach crawl, and I turned to look at Jessie who made a face and mouthed, "Later."

"Mom! I'm tired and it's been intense. Can we just talk later?"

She turned on the classical music station and graciously stopped talking. I looked out the window. We were in Hingham driving on the one-lane road passing all the pretty New England houses. Neat yards, homes each with a unique style, some with weather-beaten wood. When we reached Hingham Center and then rode around the rotary up the hill past World's End, I began to smell the ocean. My whole body relaxed for the first time since the party at the campground where Joey… the thought of that night made my stomach twist. Then Jic's face flashed in my mind, and I thought how nice it would be if he were here.

Paragon Park loomed in front of us, the white roller coaster busy with summer fun and screams.

"What is that?" Sarah sat up in the backseat and pointed to the white tracks leading to the sky.

"Paragon Park. There's rides, arcades, fried clams, everything. We'll go."

As we rode past the park, I saw the ocean. The waves were rolling in and it was high tide.

"High tide, Sarah."

"Wow! It's so pretty."

"I'll take you as soon as we get home. In a minute or two."

Our house was a small cape a few blocks away from the beach. We got out of the car and I grabbed Sarah's arm. "Let's go!"

We ran to the beach. I screamed 'OK' when my mom said twenty minutes to eat. I didn't know what time it was or what meal it was; I just knew I wanted to feel the ocean.

Sarah and I took off our sneakers and ran to the edge of the water. It was cool and felt delicious.

I lay down in the soft sand and looked at the sky. It was that blue-grey that comes at the end of a no-cloud day. The air was still warm and slightly muggy. The sun was going down, and there were a few people lying on blankets by the dunes.

Sarah lay next to me on her side and stared at the ocean. "This is a nice beach. It feels so far away from where we were yesterday. Can you believe we were in New Mexico? It feels like a dream."

"Sarah, what do you think it feels like to fly off a cliff? Right into the dark night sky."

She grabbed my arm. "Don't you even think of it."

"I'm not! It's just…so strange. Sometimes I think it's what he wanted all along. You know, to do something big. Like when he got drunk in Austin and was saying that crazy stuff about his parents, wanting them to wake up. I don't know…maybe it was just his way of getting more attention."

"I can't imagine he thought about it at all," Sarah said, picking up a stone and throwing it. "I think it was totally unconscious, actually, just about taking too many drugs. Nothing more than that."

"Maybe." But I couldn't help thinking it was more, much more than that. Or that somehow it could become more than that, now that he was gone.

I felt someone behind us and looked up to see Jessie.

I sat up. "Hi! Come join us."

"Mom wants you guys home; she made a barbecue."

I stood up and pulled Sarah up with me. We all turned and walked back to the house.

Jessie put her arm around me. "You OK? That must have been really intense with Joey. I got calls from friends back in Newton wanting to know what was going on. There were all sorts of rumors—everything from jumping out of an airplane to getting eaten by a shark. Crazy stuff."

We got to my house and Sarah went into the kitchen to help my mom with the food. Jess and I put out the plates on the back porch.

"Jess, how come I couldn't reach you guys? I was so worried, like you got sick again and were in the hospital. Where were you, I mean, on the Fourth, before that?"

"Sorry. It's just that," she looked around and whispered, "I go to this group thing in Boston twice a week."

"Wow. What's that like?"

"It's pretty cool because some of my friends are there, you know. From the hospital. While I'm in the group, Mom goes to a parents group. She actually likes it! She talks with other moms, and some of them are really interesting. One of them owns that huge jewelry store on Newbury Street; she's an artist and smokes like a chimney, and she and Mom have become good friends."

"That's so cool!"

Sarah and my mom came out laughing. It was strange to feel happy with everything going on, but I did. "What's so funny?"

"Sarah was telling me about how you two met and how she joined your road trip. Sounds like it was a tight fit in the car! What happened to Joey's father? Wasn't he going with you?"

She opened a bag of chips and poured them in a bowl. I didn't know if it was the right time to tell her there were no parents. Sometimes she was better in front of other people, and it seemed that she liked Sarah.

"Mom, I'm sorry. There were no parents on the trip. I didn't think you would let me go so...I made up that part."

She looked at me and I felt so guilty. "I'm sorry. Things were so messed up, and I just wanted to get away! Sorry."

She had a funny expression that I couldn't read. "Well, your father and I were fighting...anyway, you're back now."

She went in the house.

I stared at Jessie. "What's going on?"

"I told you, she has friends now. She also started a painting class. And Dad's been away, so...she's happier."

A knot formed in the familiar place in my gut. "He's coming back, isn't he?"

Jessie stood up and started setting the plates. "I guess, when his trip is over."

Sarah went back in the house to help. I opened a soda and looked at Jessie. Were they keeping more secrets from me? Or maybe I was doing the what-if thing again?

"There was this lady, Lu-Anne, at the campground; she was really nice and helped me through everything. She and her girlfriend taught me about the 'what-ifs,' like always worrying that something bad will happen. That it's not good to live like that because it hardly ever happens. And if something bad does happen, if you're calm, you'll deal with it in a strong way. That's kind of what happened with Joey dying. I mean, I think we all did OK with it, I think."

Jessie said, "I have no idea what you just said," and picked up a *Newsweek* magazine. The cover had a picture of President Carter. I wondered what news I had missed in the two weeks I'd been away. Two weeks! It felt like two years. So much had happened. So many new people, new experiences. Jic. I wondered where he was. Would I ever see him again? Would he disappear?

"So, Jessie, should I be worrying about Dad coming home? I mean, ever?"

Sarah and my mom came out laughing. Jessie looked at me and shook her head. No, I shouldn't worry? No, she couldn't tell me? No, don't talk about it?

On Saturday my mom took us shopping for funeral clothes at the Braintree Filenes. I bought a simple black sleeveless dress made out of cotton, and Sarah bought a long grey skirt with a black silky shirt. The only other funeral I had been to was my grandmother's and I was three, so I didn't remember any of it. I had no idea what to expect with Joey's.

Sarah insisted on a manicure, saying her toes had never looked so bad from all the camping and dirt. I had never gotten one and of course she didn't believe me. So she was bright red and I got a purple-black color, while Jess and Mom went to a bookstore to get some more beach reading.

The water felt warm on my feet, but I didn't like her cutting the dead skin off. I was a barefoot girl from way back, and there were permanent calluses on my big toes. I watched her carefully, suspicious that she was talking about us in Russian.

"Sarah, my gang from Newton will be there at the funeral, I hope. I can introduce you."

"Don't abandon me. You're the only one I'll know except for Barry. And Jic."

"If he makes it in time." I had thought constantly about him, even though I didn't say anything to Sarah. I knew it was a dream, Jic living in North Carolina or New York or wherever, and I really didn't think he was interested in me. Still, there was that hope and something really cool to dream about.

On Sunday it was steaming hot outside.

"It's going to be a heat wave for the next few days. Drink a lot of water." Mom opened all the windows on the ride to Brookline. She wasn't even complaining that she had to leave the beach house on such a hot day.

We pulled up to the curb in front of Levine's funeral parlor in Coolidge Corner.

"Mom, I'll call you later." I kissed her and opened the door.

"I can't believe you're going to a funeral for a friend of yours. It's not right. His parents must be devastated."

Sarah gave her a hug. "It was nice to meet you. Thank you so much for everything."

We walked into the funeral home. It was cool and the lights were dim. There were people standing around, lots of black dresses and suits. A man in a dark suit led us to the guest book and we signed our names.

"Some of my friends should be here," I said to Sarah. We walked into the chapel and sat in one of the seats toward the back. There was some organ music playing and the lights were dim. It smelled like strawberry candles. I looked up front and saw a closed coffin. Joey.

"Joey's in there," I whispered to Sarah.

"Can we go look at him?"

I shook my head. "In Jewish funerals the coffins are closed. You can't see them once they…you know…are dead."

I leaned my head on her shoulder. "I can't believe this." She nodded.

"I wish we had been in a good place when he died. I mean, he said we weren't a couple, it was open, but I don't know. He was so messed up. I still think he was mad 'cause I wasn't an ideal girlfriend, or I didn't love him enough, or something. I loved him so fast and then things just changed."

She squeezed my hand. "You guys were good. Joey was the one who took the acid, Joey drank too much, remember that. No one forced it on him."

I nodded. "I wished he wasn't so wasted, so drunk and high. He was sort of…disgusting." As soon as I said that I felt awful. "I mean he was acting so crazy. I'm sorry, that was awful to say."

"Lilly, I was there too. It was awful. Just remember him before that. When you first met him."

We were handed a booklet. Sarah opened it and I leaned in.

"Joseph David Berkowitz, March 3, 1961 – July 4, 1978, beloved son of Dr. and Mrs. Aaron Berkowitz, brother of Barry Daniel Berkowitz."

There was the Psalm of David written on the next page and then a note that the family would be sitting Shiva at Joey's home after the cemetery and all week until Friday.

Sarah pointed to the page. "The Lord is my Shepherd. That's a prayer from the Bible. Why is it at a Jewish funeral?"

There were more people coming in. I was searching the faces for Jic and my friends. Mostly it was adults who I didn't recognize.

"It's from the Old Testament, which we use. It's read at a lot of Jewish funerals."

"It's the only prayer that I know. My mom used to say it to me when I was going to sleep. It's really beautiful."

I nodded. I had heard it at my grandmother's funeral.

I felt a tap on my shoulder. It was Jamie. Her eyes were red and watery. "Lilly!"

I stood up and hugged her. Billy, Ted, Beth, and Darryl were there too. We took turns hugging.

Billy stood in front of me, tears rolling down his cheeks. "You have to tell me every detail. Joey was my best friend. I have to know everything."

I nodded. "I will."

Billy kissed me on the cheek and shook his head. "Crazy Joey. He's probably flying around, watching us and having a blast. Don't you think?"

I didn't know but I nodded.

The rabbi came on stage, and Billy sat down next to me.

"Sarah, there's Barry." I nudged her and we watched as Barry and his parents came in through the side door and sat in front. Barry was wearing a black suit, light-colored shirt, and striped tie. His hair was cut short and his beard and mustache were trimmed. His head was down. His mother was wearing a gorgeous black skirt suit. She had platinum blond hair that was up in a bun. She was beautiful and elegant. His father was tall and stately, wearing a black suit with a blue shirt and a dark tie.

The rabbi said a prayer in Hebrew. Then he spoke in English about Joey. What his interests were. How young he was. A Joey who I didn't know. He mentioned the words baseball, tennis, Europe, theater, loving parents, dedicated brother, and loyal friends. I thought of another Joey. Laughter, guitar, Grateful Dead, reefer, concerts, road trips, acid, kissing, sexy.

The rabbi called Barry to the stage. He stood tall at the podium and looked out at the sea of faces.

"I'm nineteen. Joey was seventeen. He was my little brother." He took a deep breath and looked at the rabbi sitting beside him. The rabbi nodded and Barry continued.

"Joey loved life to the extreme. Everything was done to the max with him. If he liked a rock group, he loved them and had to see them hundreds of times, like the Grateful

Dead. Last summer he went to thirty of their concerts all over New England and the East Coast."

"He loved his guitar. Joey started playing when he was ten. Mom wanted to give him lessons, but he insisted on learning himself. So he went to Cambridge Commons and started jamming with the musicians. He picked up the guitar that way. Joey loved meeting new people, going to new places, going on adventures."

"This summer was great for him. He wanted to go on a road trip all year. In New Mexico he seemed the happiest. He loved the fresh air, the woods, the people, he really... well, he let loose. Mom, Dad, he was really happy there."

Barry looked at the front row. His father had his arm around his mother, holding her tightly. Barry looked at us in the back. Sarah and I waved at the same time and he smiled, nearly laughed.

"Joey's friends are here. His family. All his loved ones. And somehow, I think he knows this, and Joey would be happy. He's probably playing his guitar and eating Oreo cookies. I'm going to miss my kid brother." He put his head down. The rabbi stood up and led Barry off the stage.

The rabbi said some more prayers in Hebrew. The depressing music started again and people stood up. It was a crush of people. We moved out of the chapel with the crowd, some whispering, and some crying. Sarah held my hand as we walked outside.

The sun was beating down and it was steamy hot. I blew some air onto my forehead. "What do we do now?" Sarah was still whispering.

"I don't know. Here comes Barry."

Barry came over to us and we hugged him. His eyes were red.

"Hey, it's so good to see you. It's crazy here; my parents have been so tense. We're going to the cemetery now, and they don't want you guys to come. Sorry, I know you probably wanted to come, especially you, Lilly. They have no concept of how important you guys were to him."

Sarah held his hand. "It's OK, Barry. Do what they want."

I attempted a smile. "Can we see you later?"

Barry's dad was calling his name and holding open the limo door.

"Go to my house for the Shiva. It's catered, tons of food. I'll meet you there after the cemetery." He hugged us.

"Barry, wait!"

He turned and I pulled a shell from the beach out of my pocket. "Can you put this on his grave?"

He nodded. Then we watched him get in the limo with his parents.

"What is Shiva? I never heard that expression. And what's with the shell?"

"Shiva is Jewish. S-H-I-V-A. You go to the house after someone has died and sit with the grieving family for comfort and friendship. It's usually for a week, but not on the Sabbath, which is Friday at sundown."

Sarah nodded. "It's cool. It's spelled the same way as the Indian god named Shiva. He is really powerful in Eastern meditation and philosophy. I studied him for one of my papers."

"There's usually tons of food. It's incredible how much people eat when they are grieving. You'd think they wouldn't be hungry, but it's like the opposite. The shell is another tradition, put something meaningful on the grave of a loved one."

Jamie, Beth, and Ted came over asking what was next. I told them to meet at Joey's house later.

Beth put her arm through mine and pulled me away from Sarah. "Come with us to Friendly's, we're going to hang out. You can tell us everything."

That was the last thing I wanted to do. I didn't want to leave Sarah, and I really didn't want to relive the whole awful last few days.

I took my arm away and tried to smile at her. "I think I'll just hang here with Sarah. I'll see you later at Joey's."

Beth looked at Jamie and then walked away with her, whispering something and looking back at us. I wanted to explain that it wasn't personal, don't be mad, blah blah blah. But I didn't have the energy.

Sarah and I watched the limo pull away with Joey's body in it. We watched all the cars with the funeral signs on the windshield. Soon everyone had gone.

Sarah fanned herself with the program. "Now what?"

I shrugged. "We can make our way to Joey's. There's the trolley; it's only about a ten-minute ride."

The funeral director was waving cars into the parking lot for another funeral. I saw a car waiting to pull in that was just like Barry's, a yellow VW Bug.

"Sarah!"

I pointed to the car. We watched as the car pulled into a space. The door opened and Jic's face appeared in the heat of the Brookline sun.

CHAPTER THIRTEEN

Friends

We ran over.

"Jic! You made it!" We both gave him a big hug.

Jic looked amazing. He had on a crisp, blue, button-down shirt and chinos that were pressed. He wore a black belt with black work boots, and his hair was shorter and combed back. He was really tan and had shaved everything on his face, so he looked young and fresh. His blue eyes were sparkling in the sun.

"How's it going?" He looked around. "I missed the service, didn't I?"

I nodded.

"I drove as fast as I could, but there was so much traffic, especially in Hartford."

The funeral director came over and told us to move the car. We drove down the street to a park. No one said anything because there was too much to say. He parked and we walked over to a patch of green underneath a tree. It was Sunday at noon, already steamy hot, so the park was mostly empty except for a few dog walkers.

"So, tell us about your trip!" Sarah smiled at him as we sat cross-legged, our knees touching.

"You first. Tell me about the service and what's next. You both look great, by the way. I know it's a funeral, but I've never seen either of you dressed up and, well, you look good."

His eyes sparkled at me and stayed with my eyes for a few seconds. "Lilly, you OK? How's your sister?"

I don't know why, but tears came up as I looked at him. "She's actually great, happy and looking really beautiful. I was sweating it for no reason. And my mom has been pretty nice for a change. I think she feels bad about this whole thing."

Sarah flipped her hair back. "Her mom is nice. A little narcissistic, but pretty cool for a mom."

Jic took out his bugler tobacco and rolled a cigarette.

I wanted to hug him and hold his hand. It was so good to see him. "You look really good. Did you just come from the road? How was your trip?"

He lit his cigarette. "I just came from New York City. I was at my dad's. I stopped there to get showered and cleaned up. I'll tell you about my trip, but first, what's up? I want to see Barry."

"They're at the cemetery. His parents didn't want us there. I think his dad hates us, like we fed him drugs or something. Barry's been with them since we got back. We can go to their house, Barry said, to sit Shiva; there's food and we can hang in his room."

Jic looked at me and didn't say anything, just had that half-smile on his face.

"It's kind of like a dream," I said. "The funeral, everything. Like, I expect Joey to walk up and ask if we want to get high or something."

Jic got up and stretched. "Think we can get some food? I'm starving."

We decided to drive to Joey's house, fifteen minutes away in Newton. It was funny to be in the bug again. Jic had cleaned it, and there were no more Oreos stuck on the rug, Cheez Doodle crumbs, or any evidence of our road trip.

We drove passed George's Folly. I pictured George sitting high up at the cash register with all the different flavored candy sticks, his smile and his blond-haired hippie girlfriend by his side. The patchouli smells, the incense, the bongs, cigarette paper, candles, tie-dyed dresses and shirts, Grateful Dead posters. We drove down Commonwealth Avenue past Cleveland Circle. We drove past my train tracks. I thought of all the walks I had taken, from Newton and back again. I wondered if the hobo was still there. Maybe we could stay at my Newton house and I would go to the train tracks. See my hobo, and walk. I remembered the walk when I met Joey. It felt so long ago, but it was only three months. Joey's kiss, his laugh, his soft lips. How I fell in love with him. How it went away so fast. Even him.

Sarah was asking Jic about his trip.

" I didn't stop that much, just drank way too much coffee. When I was so tired I thought I would have to sleep for a day and miss the whole thing here, I met a guy at a diner in Topeka, Kansas, whose car had broken down. He was headed for an audition in New York. I was so lucky. He was a good guy and helped me drive. Good stories too. He was grateful and said that when he made it big he would remember me." Jic laughed. "I bet he makes it; he had the look and the personality. Anyway, I spent last night at my dad's and was planning on being at the service. Just didn't account for all that traffic."

"Turn left here."

We passed Newton Centre and the Brigham's we all hung out at.

"Right at the light."

We turned onto Beacon Street and headed toward Joey's house in Waban.

Sarah was in the backseat. "You really cleaned up this car."

Jic laughed. "It smelled so bad. I took it to the first car wash I found and vacuumed it for about an hour. So what was the service like?"

We described the bad music and how Barry spoke so well and looked great, but so sad. We described Joey's parents.

"Turn left. Third house on the left."

There were a lot of cars parked on the street. Jic parked and we walked to Joey's house. It was a huge tutor with an immaculate manicured lawn.

A man in a black suit opened the door for us. We walked into to a wide-open hall. Women in aprons and stiff white shirts were putting food out on this long table in the next room. It was cooler than outside. It smelled like meat.

There were about twenty adults there already. They were huddled around the table, waiting for all the food to come out, clutching plates and eyeing the selection. We stood there and watched as the caterer put out some shrimps. One man went over to the plate and started piling on the shrimps. I guessed that was the signal to everyone else because they all started piling their plates with food.

Jic just watched in his detached way, even though I knew he was starving.

I led them over to the table. "Come on, let's get some food and go up to Joey's room. That's where Barry said we would meet. He should be here soon."

We nudged our way in. I had never seen so much food at a Shiva. The caterers had already refilled the shrimp plate. There was every kind of cold cut you could imagine, plus chicken sandwiches, quiche, different kinds of salads, dips, everything.

Sarah was by the shrimps. She called me over. "I thought seafood wasn't kosher."

"They're not kosher Jews."

There were tables set up to eat on, which all the adults were at. They didn't even look at us, and no one was talking about Joey, just about the food. It was so strange.

We walked upstairs to Joey's room. I had been in his room about ten times in the two months we had gone out. We had sex there three times when no parents were home. It felt so strange to be walking down his hallway with a plate full of food and no Joey in sight.

I stopped at his door, which was closed.

"This is so strange. It's…so…wrong. Joey should be with us." I started to cry. Sarah took my plate and stood close to me. Jic put his arm around me.

"It is wrong. It's really fucked up." He took the hair away from my face and wiped my tears with his hand.

Joey's door opened and there was Billy, with no shirt on and his long, stringy hair now down to his waist. He didn't smile, which for him was a change. I guess everyone was a little different now that Joey was gone.

"Come in, friends."

Ted was there, looking through Joey's record albums. Darryl was sitting on his bed, his shirt and tie loosened, drinking a can of orange soda. Grateful Dead music was playing on the stereo.

We sat on the big, shaggy blue rug. The shaggy blue rug that Joey and I had made love on. The third time. The first time I liked it. The time he said I was good at it. The time we laughed our heads off.

"Where are the girls?" Beth, Jamie, and Kate were at the service and not here.

Billy was chewing a bagel. "They said they'd be here later. I don't know. I think their parents are uptight about the whole thing."

"About attending a friend's funeral? That's messed up." I felt pissed off; they were my friends and knew Joey too.

Billy patted my shoulder. "Maybe their parents think we're a bad influence. You know how parents are."

I looked at my plate of food. I was so not hungry. Jic was eating and Sarah was nibbling. I put my plate down.

Billy was in back of me and took a bunch of my hair in his hands. "So, sexy girl, tell me the story. What really happened? There are so many rumors, and no one has been able to talk with Barry. His parents have him secluded. For life." He let go and sat cross-legged on the bed, picking up his bagel.

"They do not. I'm a free man."

Barry was standing at the door, smiling with his arms out.

He walked into Joey's room and everyone hugged him. When he got to Jic, he said, "How's my car, man?"

Jic smiled. "Great shape. New oil, air in the tires. She's a good car."

Barry smiled. "Man, that's cool. Thanks for driving it. Hey, everyone, this is the man who rescued my bug from obscurity."

Barry took off his suit jacket, loosened his tie, and unbuttoned his shirt. He sat next to Sarah, Jic, and I on the rug.

Barry looked older and thinner, somehow calmer. "It's great to see you guys. It's been so intense with my parents. They blame me. They have no idea that Joey drank too much, took too many drugs, even before this trip. My mother suspected; she said that her grandfather was an alcoholic and maybe Joey had the gene, but my Dad is completely in denial about his baby boy. Thinks I could have stopped him. As if I had any jurisdiction over Joey."

Sarah held his hand. "I'll talk with them. I'm really good with parents. I'll tell them what a good big brother you were on this trip."

Barry shook his head. "They're out of reach now. And they wouldn't talk with you, anyway. It's a nice thought, though."

I felt bad for him. Losing Joey and being blamed? That was so unfair.

Billy was singing softly to the music, "Walk me out in the morning dew, my honey…" He reached over and picked up Joey's guitar, which was leaning against the wall.

He picked at one of the strings. "This is one of Joey's favorite songs."

I stood up and grabbed it out of his hands. "Don't touch his guitar!"

I held it to my body and smelled. Smokey, sweet, just like Joey. I held it tightly and sat down.

Barry looked at the guitar. "Joey was going to take lessons when he got back. He met a guy from Berklee College who was going to teach him." He put his finger on one of the strings. "Joey really needed to learn how to play."

I laughed, remembering how awful it sounded when he was playing. Except that one song he knew so well, "Sugar Magnolia."

Billy stood up on the bed. "Let's make a toast to Joey."

He took a joint out of his pocket and was about to light it.

Barry held up his hand. "No weed today. Remember how he died? Come on, man."

Billy nodded. "Yeah, right, sorry man." He put it away and grabbed a can of orange soda.

Billy cleared his throat and looked up to the Grateful Dead poster on the wall. "To my soul brother, Joey. The best friend and Dead Head a guy could ask for. May he have a peaceful and groovy trip, wherever he is."

We drank to Joey. Sarah, Barry, Jic, and I were leaning against each other on the rug, close in a circle. I put my head on Jic's shoulder. They would all come to my beach house. Maybe Jic would stay, and Sarah. They would help fill that hole in my heart, the one that was Joey.

Billy stood looking out the window. "All these adults are coming in. Let's get out of here, go to Weston Reservoir or Walden Pond. Joey would want us to."

Darryl jumped off the bed. "Yeah, cool, Joey would like that."

Ted hugged Barry and nodded to all of us, saying he had another thing to go to.

It was incredibly hot. We walked quickly and silently down the stairs, not wanting to catch anyone's eye. Outside we waited for Barry by his car.

"My baby! She looks good, Jic!" Barry ran out carrying a backpack.

We all piled in and Barry got behind the wheel. Billy rode shotgun and Sarah and I sat on Jic's and Darryl's laps.

We opened all the windows. It was one of those hot July days that screamed BEACH. Humid, hot, hazy. Weston Reservoir was about ten minutes from his house. Sarah and I bounced on their laps and everyone was quiet. Jic was looking out the window, checking everything out. I was watching him sideways.

No one was talking, until Billy burst out, "Where's Joey? Joey, where the fuck are you, you crazy asshole!" He put his head in his lap and cried. Barry put a hand on his back.

"I know. He should be with us. It's fucked up."

Sarah reached across and took my hand. Jic half smiled at me, then turned to look back out the window.

We parked and walked into the woods. I walked behind Jic and Sarah, watching the flies swarm around their heads, hoping to get a bite of warm, sweaty flesh. Jic had taken off his shirt and was wearing a white tee shirt, his buff body showing through.

The part of the reservoir we swam at was secluded from people who ran or walked. It was hot and gritty out. It smelled like our sweat and pollen.

We sat on a patch of green. The boys stripped off their shirts. I took off my shoes and wished I wasn't wearing black. I wanted to swim. I thought about what was underneath. Flowered bikini underwear and a black bra.

Billy was the first one in. He stripped naked, his white, skinny butt flashing before us. As he bopped up he yelled, "Everyone in! Joey would want us to."

Joey would want us to, Joey would want us to. Well, he also would want us to do some drugs in his memory and we weren't. He also wouldn't want me to be thinking about Jic and I was.

Jic leaned against the rock, smoking and looking out at the water. Barry went in and so did Darryl, both keeping on their boxers.

Sarah had her sneakers off and was looking in. She took off her dress, exposing white tee shirt and white bikinis. Billy whistled.

Barry yelled to Billy, "She plays for the other team, man. What a waste, I know."

Sarah smiled. She loved this kind of attention. "Lilly, I'm not going in." She sat on the dirt and stuck her feet in, checking for sharks and other fish that would bite off her pedicure or her toes.

I took off my dress quickly, not wanting everyone looking at me.

Billy yelled, "Sexy girl!"

I dove in the water. It was just the right coolness. I breaststroked to where Billy, Barry, and Darryl were treading water.

Jic was next. He took off his pants and tee and kept his striped boxers on as he dove in. He surfaced right by me.

I looked at Jic and he smiled. "Just like old times," he said.

"I like your haircut and I'm happy to see your face." I closed my eyes. I'm such a weirdo.

He didn't seem to mind. "Thanks, your face is pretty nice too."

We all floated on our backs looking up at the sky as Sarah sat and watched us. Flies were buzzing in the heat and a light haze of steam held just above the water. I pictured Joey looking down on us. Billy read my mind and said, "Hey everyone, I bet Joey is looking down at us. He would love that we are here. It was one of his favorite places."

The July sun started to go down as we floated. It was still hot, now more humid, with the sun disappearing. Steam was on the surface of the water. My ears were under the water and I heard a humming. I closed my eyes and for a few minutes felt calm and like things might just work out OK. Then, like a bee buzzing in my ear, the low, sick hum started.

"What if everyone blames me for Joey's death, what if my sister gets sick again, what if Jic leaves and I never see him again, what if Sarah goes back to school, what if my dad is gone forever, what if…"

My head bumped into something. I looked up and saw Jic. He took my hand under the water. The clouds rolled above in the dimming light and they looked like all of us floating, and then all of us dancing by the fire in New Mexico, and Lu-Anne with her funny laugh and her belly-dancing girlfriend who reminded me to never ever think about 'what if,' and the lady at the fireworks with the little girl, and, of course, my hobo on the train tracks. I wondered if he knew about everything, and I wondered what he would tell me. Soon I would go see him.

41861652R00098

Made in the USA
Middletown, DE
24 March 2017